On board the *Phoenix* five very different individuals are brought together for the first time:

Alex – A quiet lad from Northumbria, Alex leads the team in survival skills. His dad is in the SAS and Alex is determined to follow in his footsteps, whatever it takes. He who dares . . .

Li – Expert in martial arts and free-climbing, Li can get to grips with most situations . . .

Paulo – The laid-back Argentinian is a mechanical genius, and with his medical skills he can patch up injuries as well as motors . . .

Hex – An ace hacker, Hex is first rate at code-breaking and can bypass most security systems . . .

Amber – Her top navigational skills mean she's rarely lost. Rarely lost for words either, rich-girl Amber can show some serious attitude . . .

Cast adrift and marooned on a desert island some-where in the Indonesian Archipelago, these five must learn to work at a team in order to survive.

Alpha Force is born . . .

www.kidsatrandomhou

CHRIS RYAN

ALPHA FORCE

RYAN

SURVIVAL

RED
FOX

ALPHA FORCE: SURVIVAL
A RED FOX BOOK 9781862307148

First published in Great Britain in 2002 by Red Fox,
an imprint of Random House Children's Books

This edition published 2004

The Random House Group Limited supports The Forest Stewardship
Council (FSC), the leading international forest certification organisation.
All our titles that are printed on Greenpeace approved FSC certified paper
carry the FSC logo. Our paper procurement policy can be found at:
www.rbooks.co.uk/environment.

Typeset in Sabon by Palimpsest Book Production Limited,
Polmont, Stirlingshire

Red Fox Books are published by Random House Children's Books,
61–63 Uxbridge Road, London W5 5SA,
A Random House Group Company.

Addresses for companies within The Random House Group Limited
can be found at:
www.randomhouse.co.uk/offices.htm

THE RANDOM HOUSE GROUP Limited Reg. No. 954009
www.kidsatrandomhouse.co.uk

A CIP catalogue record for this book is available from the British Library.

Printed and bound in Great Britain by
Cox & Wyman Ltd, Reading, Berkshire

ALPHA FORCE

The field of
operation...

PHILIPPINES

MALAYSIA

PAPUA
NEW GUINEA

INDONESIA

INDIAN
OCEAN

AUSTRALIA

SOMEWHERE IN THE INDONESIAN ARCHIPELAGO . . .

It only takes an instant to die . . .

As he struggled to swim away from the huge wave that towered over him, Alex began to hear his father's voice in his head, patiently explaining the survival skills he had learned in the SAS. It was oddly comforting to listen to that calm, quiet voice and Alex found the strength to push himself on through the turbulent water, even though his muscles were almost useless with exhaustion.

It only takes an instant to die, continued his father's voice. *The way to survive is to make sure you never reach that instant. Are you listening, Alex? You need to understand how an accident happens. Most people think it explodes without warning – blam! Like a firework. But you look more closely at that accident and what do you see . . . ?*

'A fuse . . .' croaked Alex, forcing himself to take a few more strokes before floundering to a stop. 'There's always a fuse . . .'

He blinked the stinging seawater from his eyes and looked over his shoulder to see whether he was clear of the breaking wave. He groaned. All that effort and he had hardly moved. It was as though he had been treading water. The wave still towered over him, even higher now. It was a solid slab of black water, except at the top where there was a frayed edge of white foam. The wave had reached its crest and was beginning to curl over. In a few seconds, the whole weight of that wall of water would crash down on top of him.

Alex stopped swimming. He knew he was fighting a losing battle. Instead, he concentrated on breathing, topping up his system with as much oxygen as he could before the wave hit. He felt himself being tugged backwards as the surrounding water was sucked into the base of the breaking wave. Forcing his burning lungs to take in one more deep breath, he turned and dived down under the surface a second before the breaker crashed down on top of him.

Even under the water, Alex was overwhelmed by the impact. The breaker slammed him down and knocked all the air out of him with a casual efficiency that reminded him of his mother kneading dough. As he tumbled lazily through the water, drifting on the edge of consciousness, Alex thought about his mother making bread half a world away in the kitchen he had been so keen to leave. He thought of how sad she would be if he did not return from this trip and suddenly he was fully awake again.

He began to struggle against the current, which was still rolling him over and over, pulling him nearer and nearer to the reef where the boat had broken in two. If he was dragged across the razor-sharp coral, his skin would be torn to ribbons. How close was he? There was a roaring in his ears which could be breaking surf. Alex forced his eyes open, but it was so dark under the water, he could not tell which way was up. He redoubled his efforts to swim against the current until he felt as though his chest was about to burst open. His movements became weaker, the roaring in his ears grew louder and sparks of multi-coloured light began to dance behind his eyes, but he kept going and, suddenly, the current let him go. He broke surface and pulled whooping breaths of air into his lungs.

Clearing his eyes, he peered about him. The moon was up and, in its pale light, he could just see the dark, jagged outline of the island he was trying to reach. He turned in the water and saw white surf breaking on the reef behind him. It was still too close for comfort and another huge wave was beginning to build. Gritting his teeth, Alex started to swim again, scanning the water for any sign of the rest of A-Watch.

He spotted Amber first, way ahead of him. She had nearly reached the island and was swimming strongly. Behind Amber, but still in the quieter waters of the lagoon, two more heads bobbed close together in the water. Paulo and Li, thought Alex, guessing that Paulo would not leave Li's side if he could help it. But where was Hex? Alex felt a chill run through him as he remembered that Hex, the fifth member of A-Watch, had been even nearer to the reef before the wave hit.

Despite the next breaker building behind him, Alex slowed and turned to scan the surface for Hex. He half-expected to see a body, floating face down in a spreading circle of blood, but there was nothing. Then he caught a movement over to his left. There was Hex, ahead of him now, and swimming steadily towards the island. He must have managed to surf in on the back of the wave that had swallowed Alex.

Satisfied, Alex put the others out of his mind and concentrated on swimming as hard as he could. This time he was nearly clear of the breaker when it crashed. Once more, he dived to survive the impact, then swam against the current that was pulling him backwards. He felt a surge of elation as he broke surface again. He was going to make it! Then something slammed into the back of his head with bone-shattering force. Instinctively, he flung his left arm up to protect his head and was caught in a grip which instantly tightened, biting into the flesh of his wrist. As he began to spiral down into the water, trailing blood, Alex heard his father's voice again.

Every accident has a fuse, son. There's always a fuse.

Alex watched with a sort of dazed curiosity as a thin rope of his own blood twisted away from him towards the surface. That must be the fuse, he thought. In the few seconds left to him before he lost consciousness, Alex imagined the fuse stretching across the sea and back in time to twenty-four hours earlier, when they had all still been aboard the *Phoenix*. That was when it had all started. That final Watch Duty, when the fuse was lit . . .

ONE

Alex knelt on the fore-deck of the *Phoenix* as she cut a graceful path through the clear, blue water. The *Phoenix* was a beautiful ship; a newly-built replica of a three-masted schooner with white sails that curved like wings in the breeze. She was a week into her maiden voyage, sailing east across the Java Sea. To the south, the island of Java made a jagged scribble on the horizon and all around them clusters of smaller Indonesian islands dotted the water. The late-afternoon sun touched everything with a soft, golden glow.

Alex had no time to gaze at the view. He was concentrating on polishing the brass fittings of the deck rail to a high shine. His back ached and his chest and arms were beaded with sweat in the humid heat of the day, but, for the first time since the voyage began, he was happy. A-Watch were nearly at the end of their latest Watch Duty and, for once, nothing had gone wrong. Heather, their Watch leader, had been determined to have a good Watch. She had set them their tasks and then spent the whole four hours circling the deck, watching them coldly like a small, blue-eyed shark.

Alex glanced at the other four members of A-Watch. Amber and Hex were both hunched over a big, metal cookpot, preparing vegetables. They were working in a sullen silence and trading hostile looks, but at least they weren't fighting. Li was up in the rigging, clambering and balancing high above the deck with the confidence of an expert climber. Alex was not sure how much work Li was doing up there, but he supposed anything was better than the total lack of interest she had shown so far. Paulo was swabbing the deck. He had started off well, but now he was absent-mindedly pushing his mop back and forth over one very clean patch of deck while he gazed up at Li, hypnotized by her slim legs and the swing of her silky black hair.

'Paulo!'

Paulo jumped. Heather was standing with her hands on her hips, glaring at him. He swallowed, then tried one of his trademark heart-melting smiles. The smile turned to a look of horror as Heather stalked across the deck towards him, her eyes like chips of ice. Grabbing the mop, Paulo moved off, swabbing at high speed and sending water flying everywhere. Alex grinned as he turned back to his polishing. Heather was tiny but very scary. She was in her mid-twenties, he guessed, which made her barely ten years older than the five members of her Watch, but she had started work aboard sail-training ships like the *Phoenix* at sixteen and she was as hard as nails.

Alex gave the brasswork one last swipe and straightened up, rubbing his aching back. He caught the tiniest nod of approval from Heather and grinned again. This trip might just start working out after all.

'Not bad,' said Heather, looking around the deck. 'Not *good*,' she scowled, folding her arms. 'But – it's a start. Now, listen up. B-Watch'll be relieving us here any minute, so let's get this deck ship-shape for them. Paulo and Alex, stow away your cleaning stuff. Hex and Amber, carry that cookpot down to the galley. Together! Li, enough of the circus act. Come down and take a bow. I'm off to write up the Watch log.'

Heather walked away and Alex breathed a sigh of relief. The Watch was over and nothing had gone wrong. He was beginning to think there might be some hope for A-Watch. He was mistaken.

As soon as Heather was out of sight, Hex dropped his side of the cookpot.

'Hey!' yelled Amber, jumping out of the way as water slopped onto the deck.

Hex ignored her. Pulling his palmtop from the pouch at his belt, he flipped it open and sat down with his back against the mast. His fingers keyed the air and he stared at the screen with a hungry look on his face as he waited for the machine to wake up.

Amber's dark eyes flashed as she glared down at

Hex. 'Look at you,' she spat. 'Junkie hacker. Can't you cope with real life?'

'Not when you're in it,' muttered Hex.

Li hooted with laughter as she climbed down the last stretch of rope webbing. 'Way to go, Hex. Straight through the heart. You win the Mr Nasty prize for today.' She paused for an instant, looking down to check out her next foothold, and Paulo threw down his mop.

'Do not worry, Li,' he said, leaping to the base of the mast. 'I am here.'

Paulo reached out his hands to her and Li looked at him with raised eyebrows, then threw herself backwards off the rigging. Flipping over in mid-air, she landed neatly with her arms outstretched and her uptilted eyes full of mischief. The thud of her feet hitting the deck startled Hex, making him look away from his screen for an instant. It was enough for Amber. She swooped down and snatched the palmtop, sprinting away with it as Hex struggled to his feet.

'You are dead!' yelled Hex and Amber laughed over her shoulder at him.

That was when the accident exploded across the deck. Still looking behind her, Amber ran full pelt into Paulo's discarded mop. The wooden handle smacked into her shins, knocking her off her feet and sending her hurtling across the deck. The palmtop flew through the air and disappeared over the side. In an instant that seemed to last for ever, Alex saw that Amber was either going to follow the palmtop into the sea, or smash her skull against the deck rail.

Without stopping to think, Alex put his head down and launched himself at Amber in an attempt to knock her off-course. The impact jarred every bone in his body and stopped his breath. For one, stunned second, he felt as though he was floating in mid-air, then he landed hard on the deck, knocking the remaining breath from his lungs and grating the skin from his elbow.

Alex sucked in air and blinked rapidly to clear his vision. Had he succeeded? He did not dare to look behind him. Instead, he looked up at Li, Hex and Paulo. All three of them were wearing identical shocked expressions. Alex closed his eyes, imagining the worst. Then a fist thumped him squarely in the back.

'You prize moron!'

Dizzily, Alex got to his knees and turned round. A relieved grin spread across his face. Amber was standing over him and she looked furious.

'You think that was funny?' yelled Amber. 'See what you did?' She thrust a grazed and bleeding knee in front of his nose. The wound looked startlingly pink against her black skin.

Alex stopped grinning. 'Sorry,' he muttered. 'I was just—'

'He was just saving your miserable life,' interrupted Hex, with an icy edge to his voice.

'Oh, puh-leeze,' sneered Amber.

'It's true,' said Li. 'Alex stopped you from going overboard.'

'Yeah, right,' said Amber uncertainly, peering over the deck rail.

'Really, he did,' said Paulo. 'You were about to follow that palmtop into the sea.'

Amber looked at Paulo, then at Hex. 'Your palmtop? In the sea . . . ?'

Hex nodded grimly. Amber looked down at her feet. When she raised her head again, there was a smile of pure delight on her face.

'Your precious palmtop . . . ?' She mimed a clownish dive and snorted with laughter.

Hex snapped. He started towards Amber, his green eyes flat and merciless. Amber grinned and settled into a fighting stance, her feet apart for balance. Hex was broad-shouldered and muscled, but Amber matched him in height and her reflexes had been sharpened by training in the sports only rich girls get to play. Years of fencing, archery and downhill skiing had taught her all about balance, avoidance, concentration and speed. Amber felt more than ready to meet Hex head-on but, before the fight could start, a wave of cold water knocked them both sideways. They stopped in their tracks, coughing and spluttering as they tried to clear the water from their eyes.

Alex, Li and Paulo all turned to see where the water had come from. Heather was standing there, holding a dripping bucket. She seemed to crackle with a furious energy. The freckles stood out darkly on her white face and the muscles jumped in her clenched jaw. She threw the bucket to the deck, where it rolled backwards and forwards with a metallic rumbling in the sudden silence. Heather let the silence grow until she had their full attention. When she finally spoke, her voice was tight and small, as though she was holding back a roar.

'Clean up this mess, then report to me on the aft-deck in ten minutes,' she snapped, then strode away without looking back.

Two

They made it in nine. All five of them had managed to change into clean, dry clothes and Amber and Alex had plasters covering their grazes. Heather was already there, stalking up and down the aft-deck. They looked at one another, then formed a ragged line and waited in silence.

Heather ignored them. She had stopped pacing and was standing with her head down, apparently deep in thought.

Amber looked at her watch and sighed. Then she cleared her throat. Finally, she spoke. 'You do know our Watch is officially over, right? Hey! I said—'

Heather's head went up and she homed in on Amber like a heat-seeking missile. 'Hey? Hey? Hay is what you feed to horses!'

'OK. OK,' muttered Amber.

'No, not OK!' snapped Heather. 'I expect you to do me the courtesy of using my name. Is that clear?'

'Sheesh! What is this? A floating boot-camp?'

Heather took a deep, calming breath. 'No, Amber, to most people this is the trip of a lifetime.'

Alex grimaced. The trip of a lifetime. That was what he had thought when he found out about the Phoenix Project nearly a year ago. A crew of young people from all over the world were to be brought together aboard the *Phoenix* to take part in the first of a series of eco-voyages. It was to be a special crew. The successful applicants would have to be fit, speak English and have a variety of useful background skills. The advert stressed that this was to be a working voyage, but it didn't sound much like work to Alex. The chosen crew would be surveying and recording the variety of plants, animals and sea-life to be found in the Indonesian Archipelago. They would spend the summer sailing amongst the thousands of tiny island groups dotted around the Java Sea, dropping anchor every few days to explore a new island and dive on its surrounding reefs.

It sounded wonderful. Alex had fired off an application and was thrilled when he was invited to join the crew. It had taken him the whole of a long Northumbrian winter to raise enough money to pay for his place on the *Phoenix*. He had spent his evenings writing to local businesses, asking for sponsorship. His weekends had been taken up with whatever casual work he could find. He had cleaned holiday cottages and cleared snow from driveways in sub-zero temperatures. For two gruelling weeks in December, he had felled Christmas trees non-stop until there were blisters the size of saucers on his palms.

Now, Alex grimaced again, remembering how hard he had worked to get here. At the start of the voyage, when the crew all came together, he had been full of excitement. It was a truly international crew. There were twenty of them, from all over the world.

Alex had particularly liked a friendly Nigerian boy called Samuel and Kathe, a German girl with a beautiful smile, but, when the four Watches were chosen, they had all been put into different Watches. He had been assigned to A-Watch and his trip of a lifetime had turned into a nightmare.

Amber seemed intent on making things worse. She was looking down her nose at Heather as though their Watch-leader was a piece of chewing-gum stuck to the deck.

'Trip of a lifetime?' Amber sneered. 'I didn't ask to be here. I wanted to stay in Boston for the summer.'

Heather raised an eyebrow. 'All alone in an empty boarding school?'

'Yeah, well, I'd rather be on my own in Boston than here with him,' said Amber, throwing a sideways glance at Hex. 'Which reminds me, has my uncle arranged my flights home yet?'

'Unfortunately not,' said Heather, grimly. 'He spoke to the skipper this morning. Your request is denied.'

'What!'

'You're on board for the whole voyage. Your uncle

thinks it'll do you good, mixing with people from all walks of life.'

'People I can handle,' retorted Amber. She jerked her head at Hex. 'It's street-rats like him I have a problem with.'

Silently, smoothly, Hex moved out of the line and headed for Amber. Paulo and Alex were standing on either side of her and they both stepped out to block Hex's way. Hex only stopped when he ran up against them. His green eyes were flat and his face was expressionless as he stared at Amber, but Paulo and Alex between them were struggling to hold him back.

'See what I mean?' said Amber, smugly. 'Straight to the violence. No discussion. Typical London street-rat reaction.'

'That's enough, Amber,' said Heather. 'And, Hex, there will be no fighting aboard the *Phoenix*. Understood?'

'My palmtop is in the sea,' grated Hex.

'Gone phishing,' smirked Amber, using the hacker's term for searching out information. 'Or, maybe, gone surfing?'

Hex surged forward again, nearly managing to power his way past Alex and Paulo.

'Amber! Hex!' snapped Heather. 'Stop it, now!'

'What's the problem?' sighed Amber. 'I'll buy him a new one.'

'You think money fixes everything,' said Hex, pushing Alex and Paulo away and returning to his place in the line.

'Yeah, right,' said Amber. 'What would you know about that, street-rat?'

'Speaking of street-rats,' said Hex, 'I read about your father on the Net.'

Amber blinked with shock at the mention of her father and her hand went up to the chain she always wore at her neck. An oddly-shaped twist of beaten gold hung from the chain. It had been roughly hammered into a coin-sized circle, broken at the base with the two ends bent back on themselves.

'He might've died a software billionaire,' continued Hex, 'but he was born and dragged up in the Bronx. A ghetto boy. A street-rat.'

Amber ducked her head and, for once, said nothing. There was an awkward silence, then Heather stepped closer to Amber and laid a hand on her arm. 'I can see you loved your parents very much, Amber,' she said, gently.

'Don't bring my mom and dad into this,' said Amber, clutching the broken circle protectively and glaring at Heather.

'But that's why I can't understand your behaviour on this voyage,' continued Heather. 'The *Phoenix* was built in their memory—'

'I don't need a stupid sailing ship to remember them, OK?' snapped Amber. 'That was my uncle's stupid idea.'

Heather sighed and tried again. 'You know what a phoenix is, don't you?'

'Yeah, yeah,' drawled Amber. 'The bird that rose again from the ashes. A new beginning. A rebirth. Well, I don't want any new beginning. My parents, they died. The e-end.' Amber stopped as her drawl developed a wobble. She swallowed, then lifted her chin and tried again. 'The end!'

'Omega,' said Hex, gazing thoughtfully at the twist of beaten gold in Amber's fist. His voice was quiet, but Amber jumped as though he had shouted the word in her ear. She stared at Hex in shock, but he did not seem to notice. He just kept looking at the twist of gold.

What's that about? thought Alex, watching them both.

'Gee, Heather, you really brightened up her day,' said Li, seeing the tears in Amber's eyes. '*Always Keep a Happy Watch*, that must be your motto, right?'

Paulo snorted with laughter and Li rewarded him with a smile. She did not seem to notice the way Heather's face was darkening but Alex groaned inwardly and took a step away from the others. He stared straight ahead and tried to pretend he was nothing to do with A-Watch.

'That, Li, is just the smart-ass kind of remark I've come to expect from you,' snapped Heather.

'Only joking,' muttered Li.

'This is no joke! Amber could've died back there! And do you know the scary part? It could happen again tomorrow. Because A-Watch is not a team, it is a total disorganized mess! The other Watches, they've made friends—'

'I have made friends,' objected Paulo.

'No, Paulo. You have tried to make it with every girl on board. That is not the same as making friends. You lot don't know the first thing about the people standing right next to you! Well, I'm going to tell you a few truths! Amber and Hex, you are two of the most selfish people I have ever met.'

Hex and Amber started to protest, but Heather cut them short. 'Neither of you wants to be here, so what do you do? You both go into a permanent sulk! And Li, you think that because you're our animal expert, you don't need to do any of the work on-board ship. Wrong! Paulo, what can I say? You seem to think you're too good-looking to work!'

Alex lowered his head to hide a smile. Heather had captured them all perfectly.

'And you, Alex,' continued Heather, moving to stand in front of him. 'First, I have to say thank you. I think Amber probably owes you her life.'

Alex shrugged and started to say something modest, but Heather hadn't finished.

'But I also have a question for you, Alex. Do you think you're too good for us?'

Alex's grey eyes widened with surprise. 'What?'

'I saw you step away from us just now. That's how you always are. One step away from us. Observing. And you don't seem to like what you see.'

'I—' Alex could feel a flush spreading up his neck and across his cheeks. He glanced sideways at the others, then straightened his back, squared his shoulders and stared over Heather's head into the middle distance.

Heather stepped back to take all five of them in with one glare, then she moved along the line, handing each of them a pencil and a pad of paper. 'You will each report to me first thing in the morning, with an essay on the meaning of team spirit. Until then, I do not want to see any of you. So, you will not, repeat *not*, watch tonight's film and you will not eat dinner in the mess with the rest of the crew. Just – keep out of my way!'

Heather began to walk away. Just before she left the deck, she turned back to give them all one last glare. 'Understand this,' she said. 'A-Watch is going to be a team by the end of this voyage.'

As soon as Heather had disappeared, Amber tossed her head and threw her pad and pencil to the deck. She stalked over to the stern rail and leaned over it with her back to the rest of them. Hex also threw down his pad and, out of habit, reached into the pouch at his belt for his palmtop. An expression of pain crossed his face as he remembered he no longer had it. He slumped down onto the deck, suddenly at a loss for something to do. Paulo and Li sat down together with their pads and started playing an X-rated game of Hangman. Alex stared at his blank sheet of paper and wished with all his heart that he was back home in Northumberland.

'I am hungry,' announced Paulo, a few minutes later. 'I cannot go without food. I will grow faint and pale. See?' He pushed the dark curls back from his forehead to give them all a good view of him wasting away.

'You know, Paulo, you're absolutely right,' said Amber slowly, staring down into the water.

Paulo blinked in surprise. Amber never agreed with anyone. He grinned with pleasure, showing all his even, white teeth. 'I am?'

Amber turned to face the rest of them. 'Yeah. We shouldn't have to go without food. So, here's what we'll do. We're going on a raid, OK?'

'Yay! At last, a bit of action!' said Li, bouncing to her feet.

'Collect up any food or drink you have in your lockers,' continued Amber. 'Grab some bunk blankets, then meet me back here in ten minutes.'

'Where are you going, Amber?' asked Paulo.

'I'm gonna see what I can lift from the galley storeroom,' grinned Amber.

'You're going to steal food?' said Alex.

Amber frowned, thinking about it. 'Nah. It's not stealing,' she said finally. 'How can it be? I mean, this whole boat sorta belongs to me. So that must include the galley supplies.'

'I'd like to hear you say that to Heather,' sneered Hex.

'Oh, yeah? You planning on telling her?'

'No.'

'Then how's she gonna find out?'

'On a boat this size?' said Hex. 'She'll find out. Do you think you won't be spotted having a picnic with stolen galley supplies out in full view on the aft-deck?'

'But we're not going to be on the aft-deck,' said Amber, smiling sweetly. She pointed over the stern rail to the water below. They all hurried to look over the rail. There, bobbing along in the wake of the *Phoenix*, was the little wooden boat they used to get from ship to shore on island stops.

'We'll be hidden down there, in the tender,' said Amber. 'That's a boat, to you,' she added, giving Hex a withering glance.

'Are you stupid or something?' asked Hex. 'One glance over the rail and she'd see us!'

'Yeah, but the *Phoenix* has a counter-stern. That means the deck level sticks out over the water like a shelf—'

'I know what it means,' said Hex absent-mindedly, studying the little tender.

'So,' said Amber. 'We could—'

'– haul the boat in with that tow rope,' interrupted Hex.

'You mean the painter,' retorted Amber.

'– then bring the rope round to the side there,' continued Hex.

'– which would tuck the tender right in under the stern!' crowed Li. 'We'd be completely hidden from anyone on deck.'

'I don't know,' said Alex. 'Aren't we in enough trouble?'

'Come on!' yelled Amber. 'We'll be doing exactly what Heather said. Keeping out of her sight—'

'– and working as a team,' finished Paulo.

Alex hesitated, looking at the four faces staring back at him.

'Or was Heather right? Are you too good for us, Alex?' said Li, slyly.

Still, Alex hesitated. It felt wrong to him, but perhaps this was what A-Watch needed to finally bring them together. 'All right,' he said, reluctantly. 'Let's do it.'

THREE

Ten minutes later, they were back. All the food and drink they had managed to collect was piled up in the middle of the aft-deck and Amber was busy packing it into two rucksacks. Paulo was acting as a look-out. When he nodded the all-clear, Hex and Alex grabbed the painter and began to haul it in, hand over hand. Li finished unclipping the rope-ladder and stood watching as the little tender moved steadily closer to the stern of the *Phoenix*.

'That's it,' said Li softly, as soon as the boat was tucked out of sight under the counter-stern. 'That's far enough. I'll go down first. I should be able to swing the rope-ladder in under the counter-stern and then jump off into the tender. You lower the rucksacks and bunk blankets down to me, then I can anchor the bottom of the ladder for the rest of you to climb down.'

Nobody argued. They all knew Li was an expert free-climber who could scale a sheer cliff without using lines. She was an Anglo-Chinese girl, born and brought up in London, but her parents were zoologists and they had been taking her on field trips with them since she was little. Li had come across a friendly group of free-climbers on one of these trips and discovered that she was a natural. The sport suited her wiry strength, perfect balance and sense of adventure. She loved climbing. A swinging rope-ladder would be nothing to her.

Amber tightened the straps on the rucksacks while Paulo left his look-out post to collect a spare length of rope from the deck locker. Quickly he looped one end of the rope through the straps of the two rucksacks and secured them with an expert knot, then stuffed the rolled blankets through the straps, threw the rest of the coiled rope over his shoulder and carried the whole lot over to the stern rail.

The gate in the stern rail had been padlocked shut, so Li pushed the rope-ladder under the bottom rail and let it uncoil. Boosting herself over the top of the rail, she balanced casually on the very edge of the deck and waited for the movement of the ladder to settle down.

Alex left Hex to finish tying the painter while he hurried over to try and hold the ladder steady. Li swung down onto the first rung and Alex grunted with effort as the ladder tried to twist itself out of his hands.

'Be careful, Li!' hissed Paulo. Li stuck out her tongue at him, then quickly made her way down the spinning ladder, stepping from rung to rung with sure-footed grace until she reached the bottom. There, she began to swing on the ladder until it was moving like a pendulum, each swing taking her further and further in under the counter-stern. On the final swing, just before she jumped out of sight to land lightly in the hidden tender, Li lifted her head and grinned up at them, her eyes alight with excitement.

'Five go on an adventure!' she laughed and they all laughed back, caught up in the thrill of a shared rebellion. Not one of them guessed how accurate her words would prove to be.

The *Phoenix* was holding a steady course and moving at a low rate of knots, so the little tender bobbed along gently enough under the counter-stern and they all managed the rope-ladder without any problems. Li had already spread the bunk blankets out to make the seating more comfortable. She and Paulo settled down side by side in the stern, Alex and Amber faced one another across the rucksacks, and Hex sprawled out in the bows with one arm hanging over the side.

'Give me food,' moaned Paulo, pretending to faint with hunger. 'Give me drink.'

'Did you get anything from the galley, Amber?' asked Alex, feeling his own stomach suddenly clench with hunger.

'Did I? Wait till you see the menu for tonight.' Amber reached into one of the rucksacks. 'Soda for starters,' she said, tossing each of them a can of cold drink. 'Fruit to end the meal,' she added, pulling out a bagful of apples and bananas and carefully laying it aside. 'But here's the best bit.'

They all leaned forward as Amber dug down into the rucksack and lifted out two of the large storage tins from the galley. She cracked open the lids and a fragrant steam rose from both tins, filling the air with the smell of roast chicken and cooked rice.

'I snuck in and filled them up from the pots on the stove while the cook was out of the galley,' said Amber proudly, pulling a chicken drumstick from one tin and biting into it. 'Still hot,' she mumbled through a mouthful of chicken.

They all attacked the food, suddenly realizing how hungry they were after four hours of work on deck. The rice was cooked to perfection and flavoured with herbs. They formed it into balls with their fingers and shoved in into their mouths along with pieces of spiced chicken. For a while there was silence as they all concentrated on eating. Finally Paulo leaned back, licking the last of the rice from his fingers.

'Good,' he said. 'Excellent. It is always best to eat outside, after work.'

'Work?' said Li, cheekily. 'You?'

Paulo smiled at her fondly. 'Ah, yes, I work. Back in Argentina, on our ranch, I go out with the vaqueros—'

'The what?' asked Amber.

'The – how do you say—? The ranch hands? The cowboys, yes?'

'OK,' said Amber. 'Got you.'

'We go to round up the cattle. The ranch is—' Paulo spread his arms wide to show how big his family ranch was. 'We are out for days. At night, we camp. We cook on the fire and the food, it always tastes so good.' He turned to Li. 'You must come to stay. I will take you out camping and cook for you.'

'Been there, done that,' said Li. 'We don't have holidays in the Cheong family – we go on field trips. I've eaten plenty of meals under the stars after a day spent trekking through some wilderness or other.'

'Outdoor meals are best,' agreed Alex, remembering his own, solitary camping trips in the remoter parts of Northumberland. There was nothing better than a freshly-caught rabbit, roasted on a spit over the fire, or a trout slow-baked in the ashes.

'Hmmm. Best outdoor meal I ever had?' said

Amber, her eyes dreamy with remembering. 'We'd been out on the yacht – me, Mom and Dad – and we found this little cove. Deserted. We had a barbecue on the beach. Man, that was some evening . . .' She smiled softly, then her mouth turned down at the corners and her hand went up to touch the twist of gold at her neck. She turned to Hex and a cruel, hard edge came into her voice. 'You're pretty quiet. Anything to share with us? No? I guess the only outdoor eating street-rats do is out of other people's trash-cans.'

The boat rocked as Hex started to move. His fists were clenched and the muscles in his arms stood out like ropes, but then his gaze shifted to the twist of gold around Amber's neck and he stopped halfway to his feet. For a long moment there was silence, then Hex made himself relax back into a sprawl. 'Food doesn't do it for me,' he said. 'Food is fuel, that's all. Something I can slam in a microwave and then eat without getting drips all over my keyboard.'

'A junk-food junkie too,' sneered Amber, but the hard edge had left her voice. The lack of response from Hex had knocked some of the fight out of her.

'So, if food doesn't do it for you, Hex, what does?' asked Li. 'Hacking?'

'Yeah.'

'Why?' asked Paulo, gazing at Hex with genuine puzzlement. 'What is the fascination with this – hacking?'

Hex narrowed his green eyes and considered them for a moment, trying to decide whether it was worth getting into an explanation. 'What the hell,' he sighed, leaning forward. 'Patterns. Puzzles. Codes. You with me? Binary. Morse. Sequences of numbers, or letters, or shapes. They fascinate me. Always have. Cracking them. Figuring them out. Finding what's hidden inside.'

Alex looked down at Hex's hands and saw that the fingers were jumping, keying the air as he spoke.

'When I was a kid, they thought I was slow,' continued Hex. 'They used to take me out for special lessons. They thought I couldn't read. I could, though. Just didn't want to. Once I understood how to do it, I was bored. So I'd sit in lessons, working stuff out in my head, cracking codes, playing with number patterns instead of listening to the teacher. Then I got into computers. A whole new, beautiful code to crack. A whole new language to learn. I was hooked.'

'So you turned into one of those sad, geeky types who sit in front of a screen all day and don't have any friends,' said Amber.

'I have lots of friends,' snapped Hex. 'Real friends. It doesn't matter to us where anyone lives, or how rich they are, or what they look like, or what sex they are. We even choose our own names. That's one of the things I love about hacking. Everyone's equal. You live by your wits.'

'Correction,' said Amber. 'You live by breaking into other people's systems and stealing data – or destroying it for a fee from a competitor. My dad hated idiots like you!'

'You're talking about *crackers*,' sighed Hex. '*Hackers* don't steal. We break into secure systems just for the challenge. We don't take or destroy anything. We write our own programs and share freeware, instead of buying into second-rate corporate software for dummies. You know,' he added, giving Amber an icy smile, 'the sort of stuff your dad's company churns out.'

'Go on, then,' said Li. 'What's the most difficult system you've ever broken into?'

'I could tell you,' grinned Hex, 'but then I'd have to kill you.'

'And you've never been tempted?' asked Alex. 'You've never gone into a system to get something out of it?'

'Yes,' admitted Hex.

'Ha!' said Amber. 'I knew he was lying.'

Hex ignored her and continued talking to Alex. 'This PE teacher was giving my kid brother a really hard time. Mr Rutter. Except everyone calls him Mr Nutter. My kid brother, he's – not so strong. He can't run very far. Old Nutter kept making him do this cross-country course, week after week. Said it would toughen him up. My brother started skipping school on PE days. He took to wandering around the shopping centre for hours rather than face Nutter again. Then, one day, the police brought him home. He'd been caught walking out of a shop with a tuna sandwich stuffed inside his jacket.'

'Shoplifting is wrong—' began Amber.

'He was hungry!' yelled Hex. 'He'd missed his school dinner. So, I hacked into the school system – and the Local Education Authority system – and Nutter's bank account. Made a few changes. Planted a few time bombs.'

'Such as . . . ?' asked Li.

'Six hundred pairs of running shoes delivered to the school with his name on the order sheet. Last-minute cancellation of his summer holiday. One month's wages donated to Battersea Dogs' Home. Next month he should get his redundancy notice.'

'Amazing!' giggled Li. 'Do the school know who did it?'

'They know,' said Hex. 'They just can't prove anything. They got their own back on me, though.'

'What did they do?' asked Paulo.

'Sent me on this trip,' muttered Hex.

Li burst out laughing.

'What?' scowled Hex.

'The look on your face,' giggled Li. The laughter was infectious. Even Hex was beginning to smile.

'I'm serious,' said Hex. 'I didn't want to be here. They only sent me because they're scared of what I might do next. As if being out here is going to stop me from hacking.' Automatically he reached for his palmtop, then remembered that the pouch at his belt was empty. A spasm of pain crossed his face and he turned to give Amber a hard stare. One by one, the others stopped laughing and there was an awkward silence.

Until Paulo belched.

It was loud, deep and lasted for a very long time.

'Pardon me,' he said, patting his mouth delicately as though he held a napkin in his fingers. Everyone laughed, even Hex. The tension was broken. They settled back in a companionable silence and watched dappled light playing across the hull of the *Phoenix*. The day was still hot and sticky, but it was cooler next to the water and the counter-stern above their heads sheltered them from the glare of the sun.

The gentle rocking of the boat started to make them sleepy and, one by one, the five members of A-Watch closed their eyes and drifted off to sleep . . .

FOUR

Alex dreamed he was back home in Northumberland, lying in the hammock his dad had tied between two trees in their back garden. The sun was shining and the hammock swung gently to and fro in the breeze, but something was not right. Alex frowned in his sleep as he felt the sun beating down on his hot face. The hammock started to swing more violently and Alex came awake with a start.

He opened his eyes, then closed them again quickly against the glare of the sun. He was still rocking and, for a second, he could not remember where he was.

Then he smiled. Of course! He was in the tender with the rest of A-Watch, bobbing along behind the *Phoenix*.

Except, the little boat was moving differently, wallowing from side to side. And the sun should not be able to reach into their sheltered spot under the counter-stern of the ship. Unless . . .

Alex sat up sharply, shading his eyes to see through the sun-glare. Amber, Li, Paulo and Hex were all sprawled around him in the little boat, fast asleep – and the *Phoenix* was gone.

'Wake up!' yelled Alex, a wave of shock and horror flooding through his body. He turned in a full circle, scanning the horizon. The *Phoenix* was nowhere in sight.

The others were waking up, stretching and yawning.

'What's all the shouting for . . . ?' grumbled Amber.

'We're adrift,' said Alex, curtly. He watched as the same wave of shock hit the other four and they all looked wildly about them for any sign of the *Phoenix*.

'That's impossible,' said Li, faintly.

Alex clambered past Hex into the bows of the little

boat and began to haul in the rope that should have still been attached to the aft-deck of the schooner.

'Who secured the painter?' demanded Amber, looking for someone to blame.

'I did,' said Hex.

'Oh, that's just great. What did you do? Tie it in a pretty bow?'

'It was secure,' said Hex. 'I'm sure of it. There's no way that rope could've come loose.'

'Well it did!' yelled Amber.

'No it didn't,' said Alex quietly as he hauled the last length of rope out of the water. He held it up for the others to see. The end of the rope was frayed.

'It is because we pulled it around to the side of the ship,' said Paulo, examining the rope. 'It must have been rubbing against something and, with the weight of all of us, plus the boat—' He shrugged. 'The rope frayed in two . . .'

'Thank you, Einstein,' muttered Hex. 'Question is, what do we do now?'

The boat rocked as Amber jumped to her feet and started to yell at the top of her voice. 'Help! Help! *Phoenix* ahoy! Anybody! Help—'

Paulo stood up too and slapped Amber across the face. She came to an abrupt halt and stared at him with a mixture of shock and anger.

'Ow!'

'Sorry,' said Paulo. 'You were panicking.'

'I was not panicking, you idiot!' yelled Amber, and she slapped Paulo back.

'You were doing the mad shouting,' said Paulo, rubbing his cheek.

'Sound travels well across water, you total loser!'

'But, there is no-one to hear,' said Paulo, sweeping an arm to indicate the empty sea all around them.

Amber sighed. 'We're low in the water, which means we can't see very far – and the *Phoenix* could be just over the horizon—'

'No, she couldn't,' said Alex, tapping his watch. 'We've been asleep for a good two hours. And – there's something else.'

Silently, Amber and Paulo returned to their places and everyone looked at Alex.

'The *Phoenix* was travelling east,' he explained. 'But, judging by the position of the sun, we're moving north.'

'He's right,' conceded Amber, squinting up at the sun. 'And we're doing more than just drifting. The boat's moving quite fast. I think we must be caught up in a warm-water current.' She and Alex shared a worried look.

'And that's bad because . . . ?' asked Li.

'Our boat and the *Phoenix* have been travelling in two different directions,' said Hex.

'And that means,' added Paulo, reluctantly, 'we are going to be much harder to find. Even if the *Phoenix* turned back and retraced her course exactly, we are not going to be there.'

'What do you mean, "if"?' said Li. 'Of course they'll come back for us!' She looked from face to face, waiting for a reassuring nod. 'Won't they?'

'Yeah, well. The thing is . . .' Amber swallowed, then tried again. 'The thing is, Heather told us to stay out of her sight until morning. And everyone else will know about us being banned from the mess or watching the film with them. So . . .' Amber stopped and looked down at her hands.

'So we won't be missed,' finished Hex, flatly. 'We're on our own.'

They sat in silence as the full gravity of the situation finally sank in. Suddenly, the boat felt like a very small speck in a very big sea. Alex remembered his father telling him that open water covered four-fifths of the Earth's surface, and it was the most difficult environment to survive in. He grimaced, then looked up and saw the shocked faces of the rest of A-Watch. Quickly, he pulled himself together. Unzipping his belt pouch, he brought out a small tobacco tin, sealed with waterproof tape. He began to peel away the tape, whistling quietly to himself and, as he had hoped, the others began to get curious.

'OK,' said Amber, finally. 'What's in the tin?'

'This,' said Alex, filling his voice with more confidence than he felt inside, 'is a survival kit.'

'Oh, yeah? What's in there? An inflatable island?'

Alex carefully rewrapped the waterproof tape around the base of the tin, then he pried the lid off. The inside of the lid was highly polished and, as Alex turned it back and forth in his hand, it sent out blinding flashes of reflected sunlight.

'To signal with,' said Alex. 'When a plane or a boat

appears.' He slipped the lid into his shirt pocket, then held out the base of the tin so that everyone could see. Inside, there was a whole collection of different items and packages, all nestling in a layer of cotton wool.

'My dad gave me this,' said Alex. 'I always carry it with me. The tin – and my knife.' He patted the knife, which he carried in a sheath at his belt. 'It doesn't look much, but this tin could make all the difference in a survival situation.'

'So, seriously, what's in there?' asked Hex.

Alex reeled off a list of the contents, pointing to each little package as he named it. 'OK. For lighting fires, I have waterproof matches, a candle, a flint and a magnifying glass. Those are needles and thread. A liquid-filled compass—' Alex stopped to hook the little button compass out with his finger. He slipped it into his shirt pocket with the tin lid before continuing. 'Fish hooks and line, aspirin, a beta-light – that's a special crystal which gives off enough light to say, read a map in the dark. Then over here, I've got a snare wire, a flexible saw—'

'It does not look like a saw to me,' said Paulo, leaning forward to prod at the coil of metal wire.

'It is though. See those loops at each end? Well, when I want to use it, I cut two sticks to size, slip them through the loops for handles—'

'Ah, I see!' grinned Paulo. 'That is good. It would cut down a tree?'

'Eventually,' said Alex.

'Yeah, right,' muttered Amber. 'Just what we need right now. A saw.'

Alex ignored her and carried on with his tour of the survival tin. 'That's a medical kit, surgical blades, butterfly sutures, plasters – oh, and a condom.'

'That's for you, Paulo,' giggled Li. 'In case you finally get lucky and find a girl who can't do judo.'

Paulo felt a blush spread across his face as he grinned shame-facedly at Li. He had tried to make a move on her at the start of the voyage. He had come up behind her and wrapped her in his arms. A second later he had been flat on his back, gasping for air. She had simply grasped his arm, shifted her weight and thrown him over her shoulder.

Alex shook his head at Li, pretending to be irritated, but secretly he was pleased to hear her laugh. 'That condom will hold up to a litre of water, Li. It makes a good water-bag in an emergency.' He took the lid from his shirt pocket and closed up the tin. Then he sealed the join once more with the waterproof tape.

'Shouldn't you keep that handy for signalling?' asked Paulo.

'It's more important to keep the tin dry,' said Alex, carefully packing the tin away in his belt pouch. 'I'll be able to reach it quickly enough when we need it. So,' he continued, 'we already have one signalling device to attract attention if a ship or a plane comes along, but we'd better check the stern lockers too. Li and Paulo, have a look, will you? You never know, we might find some flares or an air-horn.'

'Yeah, right,' said Amber, her voice full of mockery. 'Would you like to ask the wish fairy for a VHF radio while you're at it? Or a transponder? Maybe even a satellite EPIRB? Then the wish-fairy helicopter will pinpoint our signal and—'

'Shut up, will you?' said Hex.

'This is not a lifeboat, OK? It's a small, open boat which is only ever used for ship-to-shore hops within full sight of land. We are not going to find any communications equipment aboard this boat.'

'Speaking of communications equipment,' growled Hex. 'If you hadn't thrown my palmtop overboard, I could be sending an e-mail SOS right now!'

'Yeah, right,' sneered Amber. 'From the middle of the Java Sea.'

'It was state of the art. It had infra-red connections—'

'You have to be near the coast for that to work—'

'It was working on the *Phoenix*, until you—'

'That's enough!' snapped Alex. 'You two have to stop this. Understand? We are in a survival situation now. Everything depends on our sticking together. Hex, don't mention your palmtop again. No point. It's gone. Amber, you need to stop being so negative.'

'I'm only saying, they won't find anything,' muttered Amber.

'Found something,' called Li. She pulled a plastic sack from the locker. It was full of lumpy shapes and thudded heavily onto the boards in the bottom of the boat. Alex leaned forward as Li struggled with the knot which tied the neck of the sack. Maybe, just maybe, they were in luck.

'This must be one of your knots, Paulo,' said Li, still struggling to untie the sack.

'Ah, yes,' said Paulo, rubbing his nose in embarrassment. 'That is one of my knots.'

'You untie it then,' said Li, shoving the sack towards him.

'No need,' said Paulo. 'I know what is in there.'

'What?' asked Alex, feeling his heart sink.

'Boots,' said Paulo.

'Boots?' repeated Li. 'No air-horn? No flares?'

'Our boots and socks,' explained Paulo. 'The ones we wore in the swamp, on the last island.'

'The dirty ones Heather told you to clean,' said Alex.

Paulo looked stricken. 'I did not want to clean them. So I hid them.'

Everyone groaned and slumped back in the boat.

'Sorry,' whispered Paulo. 'Sorry it was not a radio.'

No-one answered. The creaking of the boat seemed loud in the growing silence. Alex looked around at the other four. He could see that this small set-back had cancelled out the boost in morale he had managed to achieve. They were back to being very frightened but they were all showing it in different ways. Li was about to cry, Amber looked ready to kill someone, Hex had withdrawn into himself and Paulo was a picture of guilt and misery. Alex had to admit he was feeling pretty scared, too. His heart was beating fast and he could feel the adrenalin surging through his bloodstream. He knew that it would be fatal to let this sort of bad atmosphere develop, but he was at a loss for words.

It was Paulo who recovered first. He took a deep breath and sat up straight. 'It is good we have our boots,' he said. 'We will need them when we make land.'

'There is no land,' said Li, her voice wobbly with tears. 'Anywhere.'

'Yes there is,' said Paulo, reassuringly. 'This whole area is dotted with thousands of islands. We just cannot see any at the moment, that is all.'

Amber leaned over, hooked the little compass out of Alex's shirt pocket and waited for the needle to settle. After a few seconds, she nodded to Alex. 'We were right, this is a northerly current.'

'We're moving at a good pace,' said Alex. 'I

reckon if we just let it carry us for a while, we're sure to come across an island group. And when we do, we can row ashore.'

Alex pointed to the oars, which were tucked under the thwarts on one side of the boat and smiled at Li. She tried a wobbly smile in return.

'In the meantime,' said Paulo, calmly, 'we have Amber as our navigator, but we need a leader. Alex, you have a good survival knowledge, yes?'

'My dad taught me a lot,' said Alex. 'He's in the SAS.'

'Then I nominate you as our leader for now,' said Paulo. He looked questioningly at the other three and, one by one, they nodded their agreement.

Alex looked around the little boat. 'First,' he said, 'we need to get organized. Li, store that sack of boots back in the locker. Hex, get that painter coiled and stowed away too. Amber, you fold the bunk blankets and store them with the boots for now. Paulo, you and I are going to unload these rucksacks to see what we have left in the way of supplies.'

'Maybe we could rig up some shade from the sun with one of these blankets,' suggested Li.

Alex looked around, assessing the situation. Everyone was dressed in shirts, shorts and deck shoes and only he and Hex were wearing caps. It was true that they were all well used to the tropical sun after a week on the *Phoenix*, but an open boat offered no shade at all. Everyone was sweating hard in the humid heat and losing precious moisture. He nodded. 'Good idea. You could wedge the end of one of the oars under the stern thwart and then drape the blanket over it.'

They set about their tasks willingly, glad to be busy. The rucksacks yielded three cans of lemonade, a large plastic bottle of water, a bagful of apples and bananas and a box of cereal bars. Alex put the food into one rucksack and the drink into the other, while Paulo checked the contents of the two storage tins.

'We still have some rice in there,' he said, handing the tin to Alex. 'All the chicken has gone, though.'

Alex bent to pack the rice tin into the food rucksack and Paulo emptied the chicken bones from the other tin into the sea.

'It is a good container,' said Paulo, waving the empty tin. 'I will give it a wash.'

Paulo leaned far out over the side and dipped the

tin into the sea. A rush of water gushed in to fill it, taking him by surprise. The tin started to sink and Paulo lunged forward to get a better hold on it. The little boat rocked violently as he lost his balance and started to topple overboard.

'Careful!' said Alex, grabbing Paulo by the back of his T-shirt. Amber plunged her arm into the sea and took hold of the lid of the submerged tin before Paulo lost his grip.

'Gotcha!' said Amber. 'C'mon, Paulo. Pull!'

Together they hauled the tin back to the surface and something huge and grey came out of the depths after it. They both froze, their heads hanging just above the sea as a wedge-shaped snout broke the surface, followed by a gaping mouth with rows of sharp, serrated teeth. They were close enough to see the shreds of white flesh caught up in the teeth and smell the stink of decaying meat. A dead, black eye regarded them coldly for an instant before rolling up into its socket as the shark turned onto one side, preparing to bite. The snout angled upwards, making the mouth gape wider and pushing the upper jaw forward.

'Drop the tin!' yelled Li. 'It's a shark!'

FIVE

Amber heard Li shouting but it seemed to come from somewhere far away. She stared into the gaping mouth of the shark, then closed her eyes and waited to die.

Li grabbed her by the shoulders and yanked her backwards at the same time as Alex hauled Paulo out of the way. The shark bit down on the tin, crumpling it like a chocolate wrapper, then threshed violently, shaking the tin from side to side and smashing repeatedly against the little boat.

The first jolt knocked Alex, Hex and Li off their feet and they fell on top of Paulo and Amber in the bottom of the boat. For a few, nightmare seconds, all they could do was lie in a tangle of arms and legs, clinging on as the boat bucked and tilted with every wood-splintering impact. Seawater poured in on them as the gunwales dipped below the surface of the sea. They scrambled to brace their feet against the side of the boat and threw their weight backwards, desperate to stop the boat from capsizing and tipping them into the water. For what seemed like an age, the boat hung in the balance, then it slammed back down into the water and instantly began tilting the other way, towards the shark.

The gunwales dipped down and more water poured in on them as the shark threshed the sea into a churning foam. It seemed certain that the boat would go over, throwing them to their deaths.

Then suddenly, the threshing stopped. The boat righted itself and wallowed low in the water as the great dorsal fin of the shark rose out of the sea and glided past. It was close enough for them to pick out the scars and nicks and parasitic worms that were scattered across the fin. The tough hide of the shark scraped against the boat like sandpaper as it swam past. They lay in the shuddering boat, holding their breath and listening as the whole length of the shark scraped against the wood. Just as it seemed the shark would go on for ever, the scraping stopped.

Slowly, they sat up, then kneeled in the water-filled boat and peered over the side. The shark – and the storage tin – had completely disappeared. Shakily, they clambered to their feet and collapsed onto the wooden seats. Everyone was dripping wet and shivering with shock. Hex was bleeding from a cut above his eyebrow and the red blood stood out sharply against his white face.

'*Dios Mio*,' whispered Paulo.

'*Carcharodon carcharias*,' said Li, faintly.

'What did you call it?' asked Alex.

'That's its Latin name,' said Li. 'It was a great white shark.'

'A great white?' moaned Amber.

'It was a big one,' said Li. 'Must've been over four metres long.'

'Where on earth did it come from?' said Hex, scanning the empty sea. 'And where did it go?'

'I'm not sure it has gone,' said Li, grimly. 'They

come to hunt in warm-water currents like this one, because there's always plenty of food here. My guess is, it's been following us, trying to decide what we are. When Paulo emptied the chicken bones over the side, it caught the scent of meat and decided we must be food.'

'I think I'm going to be sick,' gulped Amber, scrabbling for the side of the boat.

Li's eyes sharpened. She grabbed Amber by the shoulders and turned her away from the side. 'No! You mustn't be sick. Not into the sea. Sharks have a fantastic sense of smell. They can pick up the tiniest trace of something interesting, even if it's miles away.'

Li stared into Amber's eyes, willing her not to be sick. Amber swallowed convulsively several times, then her shoulders relaxed and a look of relief crossed her face. 'I'm OK now,' she said.

'Well done,' said Li, giving Amber a smile. 'The last thing we want is that monster coming back.'

'Yeah,' said Alex, leaning over the side to look at the damage to the boat. The bows were dented and splintered and the paint had been scraped away all along the side. 'I don't think we would survive a second attack.'

'Oh, that wasn't a proper attack,' said Li. 'It was going for the storage tin, not the boat.'

'But what about the way it was bashing against the side?' asked Paulo.

'That's instinctive,' said Li. 'Once a shark clamps its teeth down on something, it shakes its head from side to side. The teeth act like a saw, cutting through the flesh so the shark can tear off a big chunk—'

'Whoa! Too much detail!' protested Paulo.

Li blinked. 'Sorry,' she said. Sifting through her vast knowledge of wildlife and pulling out shark titbits had kept the shock at bay. Now, with nothing to fill her mind, the fear came flooding in and she shrank down in her seat, hunching her shoulders.

'What if it comes back?' demanded Amber.

There was a silence as they all thought about that. Alex stood up to get a better view of the surrounding sea while Hex sat in his place and leaned over the side of the boat to inspect the damage.

'What are the odds?' asked Alex, looking questioningly at Li.

'It probably won't,' said Li, finally. 'That tin must've been disappointing food for a shark – and there's nothing else here to attract it . . .'

She tailed off and stared in horror at Hex, who was still leaning over the side of the boat, looking at the damage. Time seemed to slow down as she watched a bright bead of blood fall from the cut above his eyebrow and drop into the sea. A second bead dropped, then a third as slowly, slowly, she drew a breath and opened her mouth to shout.

'Hex! Get back!' she screamed.

Hex jumped and pulled back into the boat, looking about him wildly.

'Blood!' shouted Li. 'Blood from your head! In the water!'

Hex lifted a hand to his head, then stared at his fingers wonderingly as they came away red. 'I didn't know,' he said.

'But it was only a few drops,' said Paulo. 'A few little drops in a great big sea. The shark, it will not notice—'

'Oh, yes it will,' interrupted Li. 'A shark is a – a hunting machine and it hunts by smell. Most of its brain is devoted to picking up and tracking the scent of prey. To a shark, a few drops of blood are like a very loud dinner-bell.'

'And we're the dish of the day,' said Hex.

Silence fell as they huddled together in the water-logged boat. Nobody moved, except for the constant turning of their heads as they scanned the water. The sea remained empty and quiet.

'I think we got away with it,' said Alex, eventually. He took off his cap and was about to start bailing out the boat when there was a splash behind them. Alex felt his heart jump as he turned to face the stern. The crushed storage tin was bobbing on the surface. Amber began to moan and Paulo put an arm around her shoulders, trying to comfort her.

'Any advice, Li?' said Alex, getting to his feet and searching the water around the boat.

Li reached down and pulled the oars out from under the seats. She threw one to Alex and gripped the other firmly with both hands. All her earlier fear had disappeared now that she had something to do.

'If it comes for us, try to whack it hard across the snout,' she said. 'Their snouts are like one big radar device for picking up vibrations, pressure changes and magnetic fields. A good whack might just deter it.'

'OK,' said Alex.

'Oh, and if we can, we should wait until it turns onto its side,' said Li. 'Then aim for the underside of the snout. That's the most sensitive part.'

'There it is,' said Hex, tightly, as the triangular dorsal fin rose out of the sea, cutting a path through the water. Under the surface, they could just make out the huge, grey bulk of the shark in the clear water as it circled closer and closer to the boat. Li groaned as she watched the circling pattern.

'What?' asked Alex.

'That circling is classic hunting behaviour. It means the shark is going to attack the boat,' said Li. 'This time, it's for real.'

'Then let's be ready for it,' said Alex, simply.

Alex and Li took up their positions, one in the bows and one in the stern, and stood with their feet apart for balance. The other three braced themselves across the bottom of the boat, feet against one side and shoulders against the other. The shark circled in, coming closer and closer.

Li pushed her oar out over the side of the boat and began smacking the water with the flat of the paddle. She knew that if the shark decided to charge the stern or the bow of the boat, they wouldn't stand a chance. Their only hope was that it would come alongside to attack.

'It's working!' she gasped as the shark turned slightly, heading towards the smacking noise. 'Get ready!'

The shark suddenly picked up speed and lifted its head out of the water as it came alongside. Again, they found themselves staring into its dead, black eye before it rolled and opened its jaws wide, preparing to bite.

'Now!' yelled Li. She brought the oar down across the snout of the huge shark with a resounding crack. An instant later, Alex did the same. The shark shuddered, then reared its head and clamped down on Alex's oar, ripping it out of his hands. They all heard the crack of splintering wood as the shark's teeth sliced the oar into three pieces. Then the shark dived, leaving the broken pieces of oar floating on the surface. The boat rocked in the wake of the shark's passing then gradually settled back into a heavy-bottomed wallowing.

They waited.

And waited.

The surface of the sea remained undisturbed.

'I think we did it,' said Li, finally, turning to the others with a hesitant smile.

'We did?' said Amber, clambering shakily to her feet.

Paulo jumped up, punched the air and cheered. He clapped Alex on the back, hugged Amber and Li, then pulled Hex to his feet and hugged him too.

Hex rolled his eyes at Paulo's behaviour, but his usually serious face was creased into a grin. Alex looked at the others, then shook his head and laughed out loud. It was ridiculous to be so happy when they were up to their shins in seawater, adrift in an open boat with only one oar, but he couldn't help it. None of them could. They had pulled together as a team when it mattered – and they had survived.

Six

Hex grimaced as Paulo worked on the cut over his eye, but he did not flinch.

'It is deep,' said Paulo as he applied the second butterfly suture from Alex's survival kit. 'But it is clean and there are no ragged edges.'

'Looks as though you know what you're doing,' said Alex, peering over his shoulder.

'I have done this many times,' answered Paulo. 'When we are out with the cattle, sometimes we are days from help. So,' he shrugged, 'we must tend our own wounds.' Paulo finished and sat back to inspect his work. The sutures had pulled the edges of the wound together neatly and the bleeding had almost stopped. He grinned at Hex. 'It should heal with hardly a scar.'

Alex nodded in agreement. 'You'll live,' he said to Hex.

'Are you sure about that?' Hex replied, looking around him with a wry smile.

'Hey, we just won a fight with a shark,' said Alex as he packed away his survival tin. 'Of course I'm sure.'

Li was assigned the first Watch Duty, and she sat in the bows, dividing her time between scanning the sea for any sign of a grey dorsal fin and searching the horizon for land, a plane or a ship. The other four set to work bailing out the boat, using their caps or their cupped hands. They had shipped a lot of water during the shark attack and it was a long, back-breaking job to scoop it all out again. Finally, Alex called a halt and they all stared into the bottom of the boat, watching for any sign of a leak.

'I think we are lucky,' said Paulo as the seconds ticked by and the boat remained dry.

Amber raised her perfectly plucked eyebrows. 'You call this lucky?' she said.

Paulo nodded seriously. 'The shark did not breach the hull. The boat is still watertight. We are lucky.'

'And here's another piece of luck,' grunted Alex as he yanked the rucksacks out from under the stern seats, where they had become wedged during the struggle with the shark. 'We didn't lose our supplies overboard.'

Hex and Alex sorted through the rucksacks while Amber and Paulo hauled the sopping bunk blankets from the stern lockers and wrung them out over the side as best they could. Paulo leaned the remaining oar against the stern seats, wedging the bottom end in the stern locker, then he and Amber draped blankets over the oar to create an awning. They crawled under the blankets and sat down, relieved to get out of the sun at last.

Hex and Alex unloaded the drinks rucksack first. The large plastic bottle of water and two of the lemonade cans were undamaged, but the third can was badly dented. Alex left that out to one side when they packed the other drinks away again. Inside the food rucksack, the cardboard box holding the cereal bars had disintegrated, but each bar was still dry inside its own individual foil wrapper. The apples and bananas were wet, bruised and battered but still edible.

'Could've been worse,' said Alex, looping the painter through the handles of both rucksacks and tying them together with a secure knot. He then clambered from the bows to the stern, looping and securing the painter around each seat as he went.

'Safety line,' he said, briefly, in answer to Hex's questioning look.

'In case of what?' demanded Hex, suspiciously.

'Rough seas. Or another shark attack,' said Amber, smiling when she saw the look of alarm on his face.

'It's just a standard safety measure,' answered Alex, mildly, giving Amber a warning look. 'I should've done it before this, really.'

'Can someone take over the Watch now?' called Li from the bows. She pressed her hands over her eyes. 'I'm getting a bit sun-blind here.'

'Oh, yeah,' muttered Amber from beneath the awning. 'Wait till all the real work's done before you ask to be relieved, why don't you?'

'You think standing watch is easy?' snapped Li, turning to glare at Amber. Everyone could see that her eyes were red and watery with the strain.

Amber opened her mouth to argue, but Alex interrupted her. 'Li's right,' he said. 'Watch Duty is tiring, especially when the sun's reflecting off the sea and there's so much to look out for. We should start a watch rota – half an hour each. Who wants to go next?'

Amber scowled, reluctant to leave her shady spot. 'Well I hope you don't expect me—' she began, then stopped as Hex clambered to his feet. He gave Amber a disgusted look as he pulled a pair of designer frames from his belt pouch and moved into the bows to take over from Li.

'Here, Li. Sit here,' said Paulo, giving up his place in the shade for her.

'Thanks,' said Li gratefully, sitting down with a sigh and working the knots from her shoulders.

'You can have the first drink, Li,' said Alex, nodding to the dented lemonade can.

Li picked up the can and the others all turned to watch, suddenly aware of how thirsty they were. She tapped the top a few times to make the bubbles subside, then eased back the ring-pull until the seal cracked with a hiss. Once she was sure the drink was not going to foam out uncontrollably, Li pulled the ring all the way back.

'How much?' she asked, glancing at Alex. 'A couple of mouthfuls?'

Alex nodded. Li licked her lips as she watched a tiny fountain of bubbles fizz out of the top of the can, then she closed her eyes and took two deep swallows. She would never have believed that warm lemonade could taste so wonderful. Quickly, she handed the can on to Paulo before she was tempted to take more than her share. The can was passed from hand to hand as carefully as though it were a golden chalice. Amber was last. She drained the can then held it upside down over her open mouth, shaking out the last drops.

'That was nowhere near enough,' she announced, dropping the can in the bottom of the boat. 'We should crack another one.'

Alex shook his head as he picked up the empty can and stowed it away in the rucksack. 'We need to ration our drinking, until we're sure we can get more,' he said.

'OK,' sighed Amber. 'Food then, I need some food.'

'It's best not to,' said Alex. 'If you eat, then you have to digest the food – and that uses up more fluid.'

Amber scowled. 'I said, I need some food! C'mon! We can eat the fruit. There's plenty of fluid in fruit. And anyway, it won't last, all battered and bruised like that.'

Alex hesitated, looking around at the others. They were all gazing at him uncertainly and sending hungry glances at the food rucksack. Too late, he realized he should have explained all this earlier, instead of assuming they would all go along with a rationing system. Besides, Amber had a point about the bruised fruit. He felt his own stomach clench with hunger at the thought of biting into an apple.

Amber saw the indecision on his face and moved in for the kill. 'C'mon, Alex! Hand it over! We only made you captain, not the boss of, like, the whole world.'

'I'm not the boss—' began Alex.

'Well, then. Give.' Amber held out her hand, palm upwards, and waggled her fingers at him.

'– but I do know about survival situations,' continued Alex, ignoring the interruption. 'And my advice in this situation is that we don't eat and we ration water.'

Amber lunged for the rucksack and Alex shoved it further behind him. She glared at him furiously. 'OK. Great. You think you're such a Boy Scout? You think you know what you're doing? Did you ever even look at the nautical charts on the *Phoenix*? I don't think so.'

'What are you getting at, Amber?' asked Li.

'If he had looked at the charts, he would know we're in big trouble here.'

Alex yanked open the rucksack and pulled out the bag of fruit. 'You win,' he said tightly, dumping the bag at Amber's feet. 'Just shut up and eat, will you?'

'So,' said Amber, softly. 'You do know.'

'I said, shut up!' snapped Alex.

'Hang on a minute,' said Hex. 'We're not babies here. If there's bad news, we need to be told.'

Alex folded his arms and glared at Amber. She lifted her chin defiantly. 'I sail a lot. I'm a good navigator,' she said. 'Charts are my thing. I studied those charts on the *Phoenix* pretty closely and, well, the thing is, the further north we drift, the less likely we are to see a ship or a plane. We're drifting into a dead zone, see? No regular plane traffic, no shipping lanes, no trade routes. Nothing.'

'There are islands, though,' said Alex, looking around at the scared faces of the other three.

'All uninhabited,' retorted Amber.

'That's enough,' said Alex, watching Li's eyes grow big with fear, but Amber could not seem to stop.

'And in case you hadn't noticed,' she said, her voice high with barely controlled panic, 'the sun is getting lower in the sky. It'll be dark in another two hours. Even if we do come close to an island, the chances are we'll drift right by it without even realizing!'

'Well done, Amber,' sighed Alex. 'I'm sure everyone feels much happier for knowing all that.'

Amber did not bother to answer. Instead she reached forward and pulled a banana from the bag. Alex shook his head.

'Like I said,' insisted Amber, looking at her watch, 'I really need to eat now.'

Paulo watched hungrily as she peeled away the

skin and took a bite of the sweet, white flesh of the banana. With a shame-faced look at Alex, he took a banana from the bag for himself and passed an apple to Li.

'Any point in standing watch?' asked Hex, quietly, from the bows.

'Yes, there is!' snapped Alex. 'One little private plane, one yacht off the beaten track – that's all we need. We keep the watch going.'

They drifted on in virtual silence. The positive team spirit they had shared after defeating the shark was gone and Alex could not figure out how to bring it back. Nobody looked at anyone else. They each sat still and quiet, wrapped in their own thoughts and only moving to ease salt-stiffened clothes away from sore and sweaty skin. To start with, they all swapped seats every thirty minutes when the watch changed, so that everyone had some time sitting in the shade of the awning. After a while, as the sun dipped towards the sea and the air cooled, they stopped bothering.

Alex fell into a troubled doze and dreamed that he was in the water with the shark, watching its dead, black eye come closer and closer. Then something came up behind him and grabbed his shoulder. Instantly, Alex was awake and twisting to fight whatever had caught him.

'Sorry,' whispered Paulo from the bows. 'But there is something.' He took his hand from Alex's shoulder to point ahead of the boat. Alex stood up and searched the sea for the shark. 'Where? Where is it?' he demanded.

'No. Further away,' said Paulo, pointing to the northern horizon. 'I think I can see—'

'What?'

'Land,' said Paulo, simply.

SEVEN

They sat in the boat and gazed at the island ahead of them. It was typical of the smaller Indonesian islands they had already visited on the voyage. There was a volcanic peak rising steeply and narrowing to a blunted point at the top, giving the island a shape like a battered witch's hat against the reddening sky. Lush rainforest, fed by the monsoon rains of the area, darkened the lower slopes of the mountain. The forest spread downwards and outwards to form a wide green brim, fringed with mangrove swamps and lagoons. It was nothing like the gently sloping paradise of white sand and palm trees that most people imagine a tropical island to be, but at least it was land, and that was just what they needed right now.

'Active or extinct?' asked Hex, gazing at the flattened tip of the volcanic peak.

'Hard to tell from here,' said Li. 'But my guess is it's extinct, or at least dormant. I can't see any smoke or steam near the top and the sides are well covered with undergrowth – no fresh lava channels.'

'There are reefs,' said Paulo, briefly, noting the white frill of sea around the island. 'And that must be big surf if we can see it this far off. It will be difficult to land.'

'Slow down, cowboy,' muttered Amber, staring down at Alex's compass. 'Don't get ahead of yourself.' She paused, squinting up at the island again. 'Let's just see if we can reach it first. OK?'

They waited in silence while Amber frowned and muttered her way through her calculations, judging distances, speed of drift and the direction of the current.

'Hmmm,' she said, finally. 'There's good news and

bad news. The good news is, as long as this current doesn't change direction, we should drift very close to the eastern tip of the island.'

Li let out a relieved breath. 'Just as well,' she said, sweeping an arm around the empty horizon. 'Because it's the only land in sight.'

'And the bad news?' asked Hex.

'At the rate we're drifting, its going to take us half the night to get there,' said Amber flatly.

'But it will be dark soon,' breathed Li, pointing towards where the sun was beginning to sink below the horizon.

'We'd better get going, then,' said Alex, scrambling to his feet. 'There's a lot to do before then.'

The island sighting had given them a common aim and they started working as a team again. Amber took over the Watch Duty without complaint, while Li and Hex tied down or stowed away anything that could be lost overboard. Paulo and Alex were in the stern, working as fast as they could in the fading light. They were using a length of rope and the single oar to rig up a sculling mechanism which would power and steer the boat when they reached the island. After a few failed attempts, Paulo came up with a type of flexible, criss-cross lashing which held the oar firmly in place against the stern but allowed him to push the paddle from side to side through the water. He experimented with different paddling strokes and soon worked out the best way to propel the boat forward and even to make it turn from side to side. His teeth gleamed in the growing gloom as he smiled and gave Alex a shadowy thumbs-up.

'Good,' said Alex. 'Well done, Paulo. Now come and sit down. We've done all we can.'

A few minutes later, it was totally dark. For the next two hours all they could do was to drift along through velvety blackness, listening to the sea slapping against the bows of the boat. Every now and then, Amber took out the button compass and checked their direction by the glow of the beta-light crystal. As far as she could tell, they were still drifting north, but the island was a small dot in a very big sea. There was no way to be sure whether the current was still taking them towards the island or gradually edging them away from it. Finally, the moon rose and gave them enough light to see the silhouette of the island, much closer now and still directly ahead of them.

'Right on target,' said Hex and they all breathed a sigh of relief.

Soon they could smell the island on the breeze. It was a rich, cloying scent, a mixture of rotting vegetation, swamp water and fresh, green leaves. Alex breathed in and was reminded of the smell of the compost heap on his grandfather's allotment after rain. The island loomed larger on their left-hand side as they drifted closer and closer, until it was too big for them to take it all in with one look. The boat inched towards the eastern tip of the island, dwarfed by the volcanic slopes which towered over them.

They began to hear the booming crash of waves hitting the reef up ahead and the sea around the boat was becoming choppier as the deep ocean swells suddenly came up against a steeply rising sea bed.

Paulo looked over at Alex and the whites of his eyes shone in the moonlight.

'Now?' he asked. Alex nodded. Paulo moved over to the stern and took a firm grip on the sculling-oar.

'In a minute, Paulo's going to try to steer us in over the reef,' said Alex to the others. 'It's going to get pretty rough, so we need to hunker down low in the boat and hang onto the safety line I rigged up earlier. Even better, anchor it around your waist or your arm if you can.'

'Couldn't we try to find a beach without a reef in front of it?' asked Li, sending a nervous sideways glance at the pounding surf.

Alex shook his head. 'It's too risky. We don't know how well we can handle the boat with only one oar. If we tried to get round the eastern tip of the island, the current might be too strong for us. We might get carried away from the island.'

The four of them got down into the bottom of the boat and each grabbed their own section of the safety line. Paulo began moving the oar back and forth with a smooth, powerful rhythm which made the muscles in his arms stand out in the moonlight. The boat turned sluggishly and started heading slowly towards the reef.

'One more thing,' shouted Alex, over the growing roar of the surf. 'If the boat doesn't make it over the reef, try to use a breaker to body-surf into the lagoon. Don't wait for anyone else. Don't try to turn back. If you get caught on the reef, it'll cut you to ribbons. Just get clear of it as fast as you can.'

The boat began to pitch and roll as the peaks and troughs of the ocean swells became sharper and deeper. They braced their feet against the hull and tightened their grip on the rope. In the stern, Paulo hung onto the oar, sometimes sculling it back and forth, sometimes letting the sea do the work. All the while he was watching the surf ahead and then turning to look at the moonlit swells behind him, trying to judge which one might carry the boat safely over the reef and into the lagoon.

At last, Paulo looked behind him one more time, then began sculling furiously. The boat caught the growing breaker just at the right moment. The bows tilted upwards as it rode the sloping crest of the wave, climbing higher and higher. Seawater poured in on them and the roar of the surf grew deafening.

The breaker, with the boat caught up in it, reached its peak and began to curl over. With a sickening, roller-coaster lurch, the boat turned its nose down-wards and fell with the breaking wave.

Paulo abandoned the oar and crashed down into the bottom of the boat beside Hex, frantically grabbing for a handful of the safety line. The breaker smashed the boat down into the surf and they were lifted helplessly into the air, then flung back down onto the floor of the boat with an impact that knocked all the breath out of their lungs. Before they had the chance to take another breath, they were swamped by the foaming, churning water. Then they were out in the air again, as the bows of the little boat miraculously rose out of the surf.

Alex choked the seawater out of his throat and took a painful breath as the boat lurched forward. He had been totally unprepared for the power of the breaker but, unbelievably, it seemed that the boat was going to clear the reef. Then his hope turned to horror as the boat slowed, stopped and began to slide back towards the reef, caught up in the pull of the retreating breaker.

'Hang on!' he yelled.

The boat hit hard. It juddered backwards across

the reef with a splintering scraping noise. A jagged spur of coral punched through the bottom of the boat, missing Li's thigh by a few centimetres. The boat came to a sudden halt and, for a few seconds, it see-sawed back and forth, impaled on the reef with the surf crashing down on top of it. Then, with a crack like a rifle shot, the spine of the boat broke in two and the last thing Alex remembered was being thrown into the tumbling, roaring water.

EIGHT

'There's always a fuse,' croaked Alex, waving his arms weakly as he tried to swim back up to the surface. 'Don't light the fuse . . .'

Someone took hold of his hands and gently lowered them to his chest. Someone else leaned in so close to his head that he could feel warm breath tickling his ear.

'It's all right,' whispered the voice. 'You're on the island. We all are.'

'Li . . . ?' Alex opened his eyes and bright daylight burned into his retinas, sending drum-beats of pain through his head. He groaned, squeezed his eyes into slits and peered up at the four grinning faces above him.

'Good to have you back,' said Li.

'Are you OK?' asked Paulo. Alex made the mistake of nodding and the drum-beats in his head exploded into dizzying pain. He turned on his side and vomited up seawater.

'Eeeuuwww!' shrieked Amber, taking a step back. 'Gross!'

Alex had to agree with her. He had never felt so gross. Every inch of his body felt battered and bruised, but the back of his head and his left wrist hurt most of all. He lifted his arm up to his face and squinted at his wrist, trying to work out why it hurt so much. His first impression was that he was wearing some sort of tight, red bracelet, then he realized that the bracelet was a strip of raw flesh.

'What . . . ?' he croaked, holding up his arm.

'What happened?' guessed Paulo. Alex nodded again and immediately wished he hadn't.

'It is a bad rope burn,' explained Paulo. 'But it probably saved your life. We think part of the boat must have hit you on the head and made you – what is the word – not awake, yes?'

'Yes,' agreed Alex, remembering the stunning blow to the back of his head as he struggled to swim ashore.

'You would have drowned, I think,' continued Paulo. 'Except your wrist got caught in the safety line, which was still tied to the broken boat. So you were washed ashore. We found you—'

'And I gave you CPR!' announced Amber, proudly. 'You know, the kiss of life and all that stuff? See, I know how to do that, because of the sailing—'

'Shut up, Amber,' said Hex.

'But I saved his life—'

'Then I guess that makes you even, doesn't it?' said Li.

Alex felt much better now that he was rid of a stomach full of seawater. His head was clearing and the thudding pain was subsiding. With the help of Paulo and Hex, he sat up and took his first look around. They were at the top of the beach leading from the lagoon to the rainforest. All around them, above the high-tide line, were strewn bits of wreckage from the boat. He tried to see whether there was anything useful amongst the wreckage, but Paulo moved in front of him and held up three fingers.

'How many?' he demanded.

'Twenty-three,' said Alex with a deadpan expression.

Paulo grinned but persisted with his questioning. 'What is your name?' he asked.

'Barbara,' replied Alex, still playing it straight.

Paulo laughed out loud. 'OK, joker. No concussion. Your skull must be made of steel.'

Alex put his fingers to the back of his head and gently explored. He could feel a crusted-over gash about two inches long. The flesh surrounding the wound was swollen and bruised, but the damage was less than he was expecting to find.

'I'll live,' he said with a relieved grin. His eyes sharpened and he scanned the others, looking for signs of injury. Like him, they were liberally covered with scrapes and bruises, but that seemed to be all. 'Look's like we'll all live,' he concluded.

'That's the second time you've promised me that,' drawled Hex. He was trying to appear casual, but kept sending wary glances into the jungle at the top of the beach. 'Do you always keep your word, Alex?'

'Always,' said Alex, firmly. 'We're going to be fine. My dad's been in rainforest like this before. He taught me all about it. It's not too hard to survive if you know what you're doing.'

'I agree,' said Paulo. 'I too have been on a trek through the rainforest, back home in South America. For one week we were walking and camping. I especially liked to learn about the campfire cooking.'

'Always the food,' giggled Li and Paulo beamed at her.

'So, you two have the experience,' said Hex, looking at Alex and Paulo. 'You tell us, what do we do now?'

Alex looked at the debris scattered across the beach. 'You can start by giving me an update on what's been salvaged.'

It turned out that most of the boat, including the piece he had been attached to, had washed up on the beach at some time during the night. The stern of the boat had come ashore with the locker doors still firmly latched shut and the boots, socks and blankets stowed away inside, as well as a coil of thin, nylon line. They had even managed to salvage the two rucksacks, both still tied securely to the safety line Alex had been caught up in.

'The boots and socks will be useful, once they have dried out,' said Paulo. Alex nodded in agreement. He had lost his deck shoes in the sea, and so had Amber. Li, Hex and Paulo were still wearing theirs, but the thin canvas would not last long in the rainforest. With good boots and socks, at least their feet would be protected.

'The blankets too,' said Li, looking around at the thin shorts and T-shirts they were all wearing. 'We'll need the blankets at night.'

'And you have your survival kit,' said Paulo, pointing to Alex's belt. Alex patted the pouch there and felt the reassuring shape of the tobacco tin. He pulled it out and checked the contents. Everything was dry. He picked out the little bottle of aspirin and hesitated, wondering whether he should take some now or try to conserve them. He decided that, if he was going to function properly over the next few, crucial hours, he needed to have a clear, pain-free head.

Alex shook the tablets onto his hand and was

about to chew and dry-swallow them when Li held out a lemonade can, filled with water from the big plastic bottle. 'Go on,' she said. 'We've all had some. That's your share.'

Resisting the urge to ask her how much water was left, Alex smiled gratefully and took the can. He sipped slowly, letting the water wash around his dry mouth before swallowing. It tasted fantastic.

'And this is your share of the food,' said Paulo, handing Alex a glossy, green leaf-plate, holding a small mound of mashed banana and squashed apple, and a cereal bar, still wrapped in foil. Alex frowned.

'You've all had this much for breakfast?' he asked. 'Have you saved any food at all?'

There was an uneasy silence.

'There's half a storage tin of cooked rice. That's all,' admitted Li.

'It's her fault,' said Hex, jerking his head towards Amber who folded her arms and stuck her chin in the air. 'She wouldn't take no for an answer, just kept saying how she had to eat right now, like she expected a butler to come running out of the jungle with a silver tray or something.'

'I see,' said Alex, mentally rearranging his list of priorities. The food was nearly gone and nothing he could say would bring it back. With a shrug, he reached for his share. He slipped the cereal bar into his pouch, determined not to eat that until they had found a fresh water supply. The fruit was a different matter. It was bruised and mashed from the battering in the boat and he could see that it would soon spoil in the tropical heat. He lifted the leaf to his mouth and, suddenly realizing how hungry he was, he wolfed it down and licked the leaf clean while they pointed out the rows of blankets, socks and boots they had laid out to dry on the sand. They had also collected a pile of wood from the shattered boat and stacked it above the high-tide line, ready to light at the first sign of a plane or a ship.

'Only trouble is,' said Amber, looking out at the empty sea, 'there's nothing to signal to.'

They were silent, remembering how far they were from any flight path or shipping lane. Their chances of rescue were looking very slim.

Alex shook himself. 'Come on! They'll be searching for us right now,' he said. 'But we're going to need some green wood piled up next to the signal fire. Leaves and ferns, too. If we want to send a signal during the day, we pile them on the fire once it's burning well. They'll make plenty of pale smoke which will stand out against the forest. At night, when we want good, bright flames, we only use the dry wood.'

'OK,' said Paulo. 'Let's get going.'

They worked quickly, gathering green wood from the fringes of the forest and piling it next to the wood from the boat wreckage. Alex made a nest of kindling in the base of the dry woodpile and, finally, covered the whole thing with the plastic sack which had held the boots. Although it was officially the drier season in the archipelago, there were still evenings when hours of monsoon-heavy rain fell after the humid heat of the day. If the dry wood and kindling became soaked, they would not be able to light the fire quickly when they needed to signal, and that could prove to be disastrous.

'Good,' said Alex, stepping back and mentally ticking one task off his list.

'What now?' asked Li.

'Shelter, water, food,' said Paulo, simply. He pointed to the rainforest. 'We should find everything we need in there.'

After a short discussion about who was to do what, Alex showed Hex how to use the flint from his survival tin and they left him on Watch Duty on the beach, ready to light the signal fire if necessary. The other four changed into their walking boots and arranged to meet back at the signal fire in three hours' time.

Li and Amber struck out along the beach to climb the headland that lay beyond the eastern end of the lagoon. They had Alex's compass and were planning to map out as much of the island as they could from a higher vantage point. They also carried a can of lemonade, a rucksack for storing any food they managed to find, the coil of nylon rope and the empty plastic water bottle in case they came across a fresh water stream.

'Remember,' called Alex. 'If you find water, bring it back to camp! No matter how fresh and clear it looks, we need to boil it first!'

Li lifted her hand, acknowledging that she had heard him, but neither of them looked back.

'Perhaps I should go with them, for protection?' said Paulo, gazing after Li.

Alex watched the two girls striding away from them along the beach, each carrying a stout stick. They looked much fitter than he felt and very capable of looking after themselves.

'Listen to me, Paulo,' he sighed. 'Li is trained in martial arts, she could climb a greasy pole if she needed to and she can probably put a name to every plant and animal on this island. And Amber – she can navigate and read maps better than any of us. What could you add to that?'

'My strength,' said Paulo, sticking out his chest and flexing his muscles.

Alex laughed. 'Yeah, well I need your strength more than they do. We'll be doing the heavy work. Come on, let's go.'

NINE

Paulo and Alex walked to the other end of the lagoon and started a systematic search of the fringe of rainforest which edged the beach. For nearly two hours, they worked their way along the forest fringe, moving in a series of small squares which always started and ended on the beach.

The trees were smaller and more widely spaced at the edge of the forest and sunlight penetrated through their branches to the forest floor, where dense undergrowth grew in the rich covering of leaf mulch. Alex and Paulo had to fight a way through and progress was frustratingly slow. The undergrowth was full of thorns and they kept a constant look-out for snakes. It was hard going, but it was also very successful. Because the trees were smaller and draped with vines, it was easy to climb up to the level where fruit or leaves grew and, every time they emerged from the forest, they brought something out with them.

When they took a rest after two hours, Alex and Paulo had gathered a good selection of supplies, which were laid out on the beach beside them. There was a bunch of small, green tropical bananas, a pile of enormous, glossy banana leaves, a few yams and mangoes, some cut vines and a big stack of green bamboo canes. It was a good result, but still Alex was starting to get worried. He had been searching all morning and still had not found the one thing he really wanted. A game trail. Once they had a game trail to follow, he was pretty sure it would lead them to fresh water.

Alex picked up a mango and split it open with his knife. He cut the flesh away from the flat stone at the centre of the fruit, then handed half of it to Paulo.

Paulo armed the sweat from his face. 'That is

enough, I think?' he said, hopefully, nodding to the pile of supplies. 'We have found a lot.'

'No,' said Alex. 'We need to go back in.'

Paulo groaned. 'I knew you were going to say that.'

'Not yet, though,' grinned Alex. 'We'll rest a while first.'

Paulo immediately settled back against the trunk of the shady tree they were resting under and closed his eyes. Soon he was snoring gently. Alex was too worried to doze. Back home in Northumberland, listening to his father, he had been sure he could survive in a tropical rainforest. Now he was actually in that situation, he felt a lot less certain of everything. What if he had already stumbled right over a game trail without noticing it? Alex looked across at Paulo and felt slightly reassured. At least the South American had some practical experience of tropical conditions, but how could he sleep so easily? Alex scowled in irritation as he finished his half of the mango. He took out his knife and whittled two new wooden handles for the flexible saw, then he took a small piece of sandstone from his knife sheath and honed the blade of his knife until it was back to full sharpness.

When he had finished, Paulo was still deeply asleep, but Alex could not delay the search for water any longer. His head was thudding with pain again and he knew it was only partly caused by his scalp wound. A headache was also a sign of dehydration. He forced himself to his feet and woke Paulo. This time, he had decided that they would plunge into the forest and keep going on as straight a line as they could manage until they found what they were looking for.

By the time they stumbled onto a game trail, they were both sweating hard and panting for breath. Their arms were streaked with thin lines of blood from thorn scratches and the mixture of blood and sweat had attracted a cloud of whining mosquitoes.

'This is a game trail?' asked Paulo.

'Yes,' grinned Alex, still slightly dizzy with relief that he had found one. 'Quite a well-used one too.'

'How can you tell?'

'See all the tracks in the mud there?' asked Alex. 'They look like deer tracks to me. And see how there are no twigs or branches growing over the trail? That's because there's a regular flow of traffic moving along here. There'll be water at the end of this trail.'

'*Infierno!*' cursed Paulo, standing in the middle of the game trail and swatting mosquitoes. 'They are fierce – and so annoying!' He grinned. 'They remind me of my little sisters.'

'Here,' said Alex, bending and scooping up a handful of soft mud from the side of the trail. 'Use some of this. It might help.'

They smeared the mud all over their faces, necks and arms in a thick layer. It was wonderfully cooling and it did seem to give some protection against the mosquitoes.

'Ah, yes,' said Paulo. 'The mud pack. Good for the skin. I will be even more handsome after this.'

Alex gave Paulo a sideways glance, wondering whether he was serious. Paulo looked back at him, his face caked with stinking mud and his eyes dancing with amusement. He was sending himself up. Alex grinned and shook his head as he hammered a stick into the ground to mark the spot where they had come out of the forest. He was beginning to like Paulo. He might have a lazy streak a mile wide, but he worked hard when he had to and he always seemed to stay cheerful.

'How long left before we meet up with the others again?' asked Alex.

Paulo cleared the mud from the face of his Rolex watch. 'Just under half an hour.'

Alex stared along the game trail which led into the deeper, primary forest on the lower slopes of the mountain. There was water that way, he was almost sure of it, and water was essential to their survival. Without it, they would not live for more than three days.

'Right,' he decided. 'We'll give ourselves ten minutes to explore the trail before we turn back.'

They had taken only a few steps along the trail when a single, high shriek, full of pain and fear, rang out from somewhere up ahead. Instantly, the steady singing of the crickets was switched off and the forest was plunged into silence. Alex and Paulo froze where they stood.

'*Dios Mio!*' whispered Paulo. 'The girls!'

'No,' said Alex, relaxing a little as the crickets resumed their song. 'It came from further up the trail. An animal. A dying animal.'

'You mean something – killed it?' Paulo shuddered. 'Do we go on?'

Alex stared along the narrow track, trying to see what lay ahead, but the forest crowded right up to the edge of the trail. Finally, he shrugged. 'I think we must,' he said, starting to walk again. 'We have to find water.'

'And the animal?'

'Animals mean water,' said Alex, over his shoulder.

Paulo hesitated, then grasped his stick more tightly and followed Alex. 'I hope the others are safe,' he muttered uneasily.

TEN

Amber shrieked loudly, then shrieked again.

'Eeeuuww! Get it off me! Get it off!'

Li rolled her eyes heavenwards and turned to see what the problem was this time. Amber was balancing on one foot in the mangrove swamp and holding the other leg clear of the green, stinking water.

'What?' said Li.

Amber pointed a shaking finger at the back of her knee. A very large leech was hanging there. It was olive green in colour, with lines of small, black dots along its length. The body below the mouth was distended into the shape of a pear, the rounded end full of blood. The leech was pulsing slightly and its glistening skin was streaked with Amber's blood, which was also dripping steadily into the swamp water.

'That's going to attract more of them,' observed Li, pointing to the pink tinged water.

Amber flinched, then turned and scrambled up the gnarled root of a mangrove tree until she could perch clear of the water. Li swung herself up beside Amber with one, easy motion, then bent to look at the leech.

'It's nearly full,' she said, calmly. 'It'll drop off soon.'

'Take if off now!' demanded Amber.

'I can't do that,' said Li. 'We need some heat or alcohol or something to make it let go. If I try to pull it, the head will come off and the jaws will be stuck in your leg. Then it'll get infected and—'

'I want it off now,' moaned Amber.

'Hey! It's your fault we're up to our knees in a mangrove swamp!' snapped Li. 'You're the one who insisted we came back this way!'

She turned away from Amber and pushed her long, black hair away from her sweaty face, trying to figure out when things had started to turn sour. The first part of the morning had gone well. They had worked their way around the coastline until they came to the mangrove swamp. Then they had headed inland, following a game trail and stopping to gather ripe, orange pawpaws and wild figs on the way. The game trail had taken them neatly around the swamp to the base of the headland. From there, it had been mainly hard, uphill walking, with one final, short section of real climbing, which Li had managed easily. Once she reached the top, Li had anchored the nylon line to a rock outcrop and lowered the other end for Amber to tie around her waist with a bowline. To Li's surprise, Amber had climbed slowly but well, following her route almost exactly. Li made sure she kept taking in the rope as Amber climbed, keeping it taut just in case, but it was never really needed.

At the top of the headland, they had discovered a tiny, fresh-water run-off, where they filled the plastic bottle to take back with them. Then they had found a rock to lean against as they rested together, sharing the can of lemonade and looking out to sea. They had scanned the sea again and again but saw only featureless water, stretching to the far horizon. There were no planes, no ships and no other islands.

Discouraged, they had turned their backs on the sea to study the geography of this side of the island. Below and to the east was their lagoon, with the reef beyond. It was the only stretch of sand in sight. The rest of the coastline was a hostile mixture of mangrove swamps and rocky headlands. Behind them the rainforest stretched like a huge green, moving sea and above them the mountain climbed skyward. Li studied the shape and contours of the island for a long time. Finally, she sat back, satisfied that she had worked out and memorized the best route round to the other side of the mountain.

'Looks like we're on our own,' she said, looking out to sea again. 'The *Phoenix* could be anywhere out there.'

'But they must be missing us by now!' protested Amber.

'They may be missing us, but that doesn't mean they know where to find us,' Li had replied. 'They don't know about the current. They don't know we lost an oar. They have to search the most obvious places first. Today, they'll double back and search yesterday's route.'

That was when things had started to go wrong. Amber had turned sullen and difficult on the way back and had insisted that she did not have the energy to walk much further, so against Li's better judgement they had cut through the swamp instead of going round it.

Now Li snorted as she squatted next to Amber on the roots of the mangrove tree. 'Some short cut this turned out to be,' she said, swatting a persistent mosquito.

Amber was talking to herself in a trembling monotone. 'I can't believe it. Ten days ago I was sitting in the Savoy, having afternoon tea with my uncle. I was wearing a Prada dress and a pair of simple, diamond earrings. We shared a pot of Earl Grey and talked about buying a house in London. Now, I'm in the middle of a swamp, covered in mosquito bites with a leech hanging off my leg!'

Li hid a smile and turned back to the problem of

the leech. 'You're wrong about one thing,' she said, looking at the back of Amber's knee. 'You don't have a leech hanging off your leg. It finished its lunch and left quietly, just like I said it would. See?'

Amber twisted to look at the back of her knee, then gave Li a weak smile. 'Sorry about the swamp,' she said. 'I was so tired and I thought it would be quicker. I was wrong.'

Li glanced at Amber in surprise. She did look exhausted. Her face was covered in a sheen of sweat and the skin around her mouth had an unhealthy grey tinge to it. 'Come on,' said Li, softly. 'We're nearly through it, see?' She pointed to the green dome of the rainforest, rising above the swamp. 'We can pick up the game trail again just over there—'

Li stopped in mid-sentence as a series of hisses and deep, grunting roars came out of the rainforest and travelled clearly across the still waters of the swamp. An explosion of brightly coloured birds shot out of the top of the rainforest canopy and the undergrowth shook as something big thrashed and crashed about amongst the trees.

'What is that?' whispered Amber.

'I'm not sure,' said Li, gazing at the fringes of the rainforest. 'But I have a feeling it wasn't such a mistake coming back through the swamp after all.'

'Why?'

'Because if we'd gone around the edge of it again, we would've met – whatever that is.'

Amber stared over at the threshing undergrowth and listened to the hissing roars. 'Trouble is, we have to go back into the forest at some time,' she said, in a wobbly voice. 'It's the only way back to the beach.'

ELEVEN

'Alex. It is time to head back.'

Reluctantly, Alex came to a stop in the middle of the game trail.

'We have walked for ten minutes,' said Paulo, tapping his watch. 'We must be back on the beach at the rendezvous time.'

Alex nodded but stayed where he was. He did not want to retrace his steps when a stream of fresh, gurgling water could be waiting for them just around the next bend. He put a hand to his aching head, trying to decide whether to keep walking for another five minutes.

Paulo waited patiently for Alex to make up his mind, letting the peace of the primary rainforest settle around him. The trees were massive here, with huge trunks supporting a high, green canopy of leaves so dense that the sun could not break through. Under the canopy, it was cool and dim, and there was a constant background noise made up of the singing of crickets and birds, the rustle of leaves and the tiny scrabblings of millions of insects. Paulo tilted his head, listening. The forest sounded busy, purposeful. He smiled. It reminded him of the hum of a huge piece of machinery, and he liked machines. Suddenly, his head came up and his eyes widened as he realized he was hearing a new noise.

'Listen,' he hissed.

Alex tensed and raised his stick, then he saw the look of sheer delight on Paulo's face.

'I hear water,' said Paulo.

They ran, dodging low branches and swinging vines. The trail was climbing steeply now and the light grew stronger as the canopy thinned above them. They burst out of the forest into a clearing at the base of a rock outcrop on the lower slopes of the mountain. Alex and Paulo stumbled to a halt and stared. Directly ahead of them, water poured from a hole in the face of the rock, cascading down to a shallow pool which had been hollowed out of the ground beneath.

Alex unclipped the pouch from his belt and dropped it next to their sticks and the rucksack, then they both ran into the pool, fully dressed and still in their boots. The water was cold, clear and refreshing after its journey down through the centre of the mountain.

'Don't drink any,' warned Alex, as Paulo plunged straight under the waterfall. He stood there, whooping and yelling as the water washed away the sticky layers of salt, sweat and blood. Alex stayed in the quieter waters, grinning with relief because they had finally found their fresh water supply. He studied the area, looking for signs that the water was good. There were plants and vines hanging from the outcrop around the waterfall and the rocks were covered with bright green mosses. The vegetation around the pool was cropped short and there were many hoofprints in the wet clay edging the water.

Alex nodded in satisfaction. If animals were using it and plants grew beside it, the signs were good. He relaxed a little, easing into the water until he was floating on his back. He looked up at the face of the outcrop, noting that there were other openings in the rock, including a cave entrance at ground level on the far edge of the pool.

Alex frowned and sat up, clearing the water from his face. There was something lying in front of the cave. He stood up to get a better look but still could not make out what the thing was. Alex waded over to the edge of the pool and then stumbled to a halt a few metres from the dark cave opening as all the pieces of the jigsaw slotted into place. His eyes widened with horror as, finally, he understood what he was seeing.

It looked like a gruesome piece of modern art. Splashes of red stained the ground, darkening to black where blood had collected in the rock hollows. Ants scurried everywhere. A sour green pool of bile leaked from a shredded piece of liver and matted scraps of brown pelt were scattered around like confetti. A nub of blue-white bone poked from one tiny cloven hoof, which stood neatly in the middle of the carnage, as black and shiny as a child's patent-leather shoe.

'What is that?' breathed Paulo.

'That is what screamed,' said Alex. 'A small deer, I think. Hard to tell.'

'But, there is so little left! What could have eaten a whole deer so quickly?'

Alex peered warily into the dark cave mouth, then scanned the forest around the pool. 'I don't know.'

Paulo backed away from the cave. 'I think it is time to leave,' he said.

'We will,' said Alex. 'As soon as we've collected some water.'

They waded back into the pool with the condom from Alex's survival tin and held it under the waterfall until it was filled to capacity. Alex tied the top in a knot, his fingers fumbling on the wet latex, then they eased it into the empty rucksack, sending wary glances at the cave and the forest. As soon as the rucksack straps were secured, they plunged back into the forest again, moving fast and silently along the game trail, checking every shadow and wondering whether they would make it back to the beach.

TWELVE

Hex was a natural loner.

Normally, he liked nothing better than being on his own. Three hours earlier, when the other four had left him on the beach, he had been glad to see them go. Now, he was uneasy. For the past thirty minutes, he had been unable to shake off the growing feeling that something was watching him.

Stalking him.

Hex shrugged and made himself turn away from the rainforest to scan the sea for any sign of rescuers. Immediately, the skin between his shoulder blades prickled and the muscles of his back tightened in protest. With a curse, he swung round again, checking the beach. There was nothing there. A branch cracked in the dark forest beyond the beach and he jumped. 'Hello?' he called. 'Alex? Li?'

The only reply was from a startled bird. Hex stared into the bushes, wondering whether he ought to go and investigate. The skin prickled on the back of his neck and he decided he did not want to go any closer.

Earlier in the morning he had been happy to work steadily along the fringe of the rainforest for over an hour, collecting more wood for the signal fire and building a second pile nearby for their campfire. Then, after a short break and a few sips of water from his lemonade can, he had picked up the broken paddle end of the oar and gone hunting for sand crabs.

He knew where to find them. He had spotted them earlier, at dawn, scurrying out of the water and up the sloping sand to their burrows at the top of the beach. Back then there had been other priorities, such as salvaging what could be dragged from the surf, but he had memorized the position of their burrows for later.

Now, Hex looked over at the locker doors in the stern section of the boat and smiled. There were four big sand crabs skittering about inside those lockers, the result of twenty minutes of hard digging with the paddle. His smile broadened as he imagined the faces of the others when he showed them his catch, then faded again as he looked at his watch.

The three hours were up.

Where were they?

Suddenly, Alex and Paulo burst from the under-growth to his right and ran full-pelt along the beach towards him. Hex hurried to meet them.

'I think there's something in there!' he shouted, pointing to the rainforest.

'We know,' panted Alex, coming to a halt and easing the heavy rucksack from his shoulder. 'We nearly met it.'

'Where are the girls?' asked Paulo.

'They're not back yet,' said Hex.

Paulo's face tightened with worry. 'I knew I should have gone with them,' he said.

Just then, a faint yell came from the western end of the beach. The boys turned to see Li and Amber running across the soft sand towards them. Their fear was obvious, even though they were still some distance away. They kept looking over their shoulders as though they were being chased, but there was nothing behind them.

'Thank God,' said Paulo. 'They are safe.'

They met at the signal fire. Amber's face was grey with fear and exhaustion. She collapsed onto the sand, too out of breath to speak. Li bent and rested her hands on her knees. 'There's . . . something . . .' she began.

'In the rainforest,' finished Paulo. 'We know.'

Half an hour later, they were all a lot calmer. The campfire was lit, the boiled water was cooling and the sand crabs were nearly ready.

'So,' said Li, settling back with her second lemonade can full of water, 'we know there are at least three of them.'

'Yeah, but three what?' asked Amber.

'Monkeys?' guessed Paulo.

'Monkeys wouldn't kill a deer, would they?' said

Alex, leaning forward to poke a stray stick back into the fire.

'The creatures we heard, they sounded big. Like – like tigers, or something,' said Amber, looking over her shoulder towards the headland.

'Yeah, right. Tigers,' mocked Hex, forgetting how spooked he had been on his own, now that everyone was back at the beach. 'Or maybe a Tyrannosaurus Rex?'

'Well, excuse me!' flared Amber. 'Brave words from a guy who was scared of a few bushes!'

Hex glowered at Amber, but she ignored him. She was too busy watching Paulo as he prepared the cooked crabs, breaking open the shells with a stone and scraping the meat out.

'Aren't you done yet?' she demanded. 'I need to eat now.'

Paulo frowned and looked up at Amber. He was about to invite her to take over, but relented when he saw her grey, sweaty face. She did not look at all good. 'Nearly there,' he said instead as he mixed the crab meat with the remains of the cooked rice to make it go further. 'Just waiting for the yams to finish cooking.'

Li was still deep in thought. 'It can't be tigers,' she said, taking Amber's suggestion seriously. 'Not on an island this small. I don't think it could sustain them. It could be wild pigs, though. They can be pretty fearsome.'

'Well, whatever they are,' said Alex, shifting the storage tin away from the fire and flipping the lid open, 'they could do us some serious damage. So we need to take some safety precautions.'

He used his knife to hook the peeled yams from the boiling water and laid them out on a large stone. 'One. Nobody goes into the forest alone. Two, we dig a proper latrine a good way from the camp. And three, we set watches through the night.'

Alex looked over at Amber to see whether she would argue with that, but she was too busy rummaging through her belt pouch. He looked at the other three and they all nodded in agreement. Satisfied, Alex mashed the yams with a smaller stone, then began serving them out onto the five banana-leaf plates, next to Paulo's crab and rice mixture.

'It looks good!' said Li.

'Don't sound so surprised,' grinned Alex. 'Let's eat.'

'It looks like Amber's already started,' grated Hex, with a voice as hard as stone.

'What?' mumbled Amber, giving Hex a startled glance.

'She just took something out of her belt pouch and stuffed it in her mouth.'

'I did not!' protested Amber.

Hex did not bother to reply. Instead, he grabbed Amber's wrist and squeezed until she whimpered with pain and let her hand fall open. Half a tube of glucose energy sweets fell from her fingers onto the sand. There was a silence as they all stared at the sweets then looked up at Amber.

'How could you?' asked Li, quietly. 'How could you keep those to yourself?'

'You don't get it,' whispered Amber, her eyes big with tears.

'What else is in there?' said Hex, pointing to Amber's belt pouch.

'Nothing. No more food. Just girl stuff,' said Amber, putting a protective hand over the pouch.

Hex lunged for the pouch and yanked hard, trying to pull it away from the belt.

'Wait! Wait!' shrieked Amber. 'You might break them!'

'Show us, then,' said Hex. He stood over Amber, his fists clenched and his face full of anger. She hesitated, looking to the others for help.

'We're waiting,' said Alex, icily.

Slowly, Amber pulled out the remaining contents of the pouch. There was a little metal box with a digital display on the front, a handful of foil-wrapped antiseptic wipes, a clear plastic tube containing a bunch of thin plastic strips and three brightly coloured, chunky plastic pens. Li, Paulo and Hex stared down at the little collection of items with puzzled looks on their faces.

'See?' said Amber. 'No more food.'

She began to shovel everything back into her pouch but Alex gently laid his hand over hers and she stopped. 'Why didn't you tell us?' he asked.

'Tell us what?' demanded Li. 'That she has a thing about chunky pens?'

Alex waited for Amber to say something but she stayed silent with her head down. 'They aren't pens,' he sighed, after a few seconds. 'At least, not the sort you mean. Those two are insulin pens, and the third one is part of a blood sugar testing kit, along with that little box and the plastic strips.'

'Insulin pens?' said Li.

'For injecting insulin,' explained Alex. 'Amber is a diabetic.'

There was a shocked silence as they took in this new information. Amber finished repacking her belt pouch, then looked at the others defiantly, blinking the tears from her eyes.

'But that is nothing to be ashamed of,' said Paulo.

'I'm not ashamed!' said Amber. 'I was hiding it because I didn't want anyone treating me differently, like I was an invalid or something. I'm not. I was doing fine on the *Phoenix*, but since we've been on the island I've been struggling a bit.'

'Are you running short of insulin?' asked Li.

'Oh no, it's not the insulin. These two pens hold enough insulin to last me another month. The problem is, if I miss meals, or use more energy than usual, I can end up having a hypo. Because of low blood sugar, see? I get all sweaty and tired and irritable to start with. Then, if my blood sugar keeps going down, I pass out and – well – worst case scenario? I don't live to tell the tale.'

The other four looked at one another, feeling vaguely ashamed of themselves.

'Sorry,' said Paulo.

'What for?' asked Amber.

'All that snappy behaviour – and demanding to be fed,' said Li. 'We thought you were just—'

'Spoilt? Selfish?' Amber grinned. 'I am! I'm a spoilt, selfish diabetic! Now gimme some food!'

Alex, Li and Paulo burst out laughing. Hex did not join in. Instead, he got to his feet and handed one of the banana-leaf plates to Amber. Then he picked up his own food and scraped half of it onto Amber's plate. Startled, she looked up into his face. Hex met her eyes, nodded once, then sat back down, scowling fiercely. Amber swallowed, but the lump in her throat would not go away.

'Don't worry, Amber,' said Li. 'We'll be rescued within a month, you'll see.'

'Yeah, course we will,' said Amber, through a mouthful of crab.

'And there's plenty of food here,' said Alex. 'You'll be fine. We'll make sure of it.'

'I know,' nodded Amber, but her gaze was turned towards the empty sea.

'Good,' said Alex, into the awkward silence. 'As long as you know. Eat up, everyone – and don't hang about. This afternoon we're going to build ourselves a camp.'

THIRTEEN

Amber sat in state under a temporary shelter of banana leaves, eating wild figs while the camp slowly grew around her. It was good to rest with a belly full of food. The grey tinge was leaving her skin and she was feeling better by the minute. Even though she was sitting still, she had plenty to do. She was keeping the fire going, gradually feeding two long logs into the centre of the flames a section at a time, and she was boiling the remains of the fresh water to make sure it was sterile. The storage tin was suspended over the flames, hanging from a stick which rested in the clefts of two upright sticks, one on each side of the fire. Her hands were busy weaving strips of palm fronds into five flower-pot style sun-hats and her eyes were busy scanning sea and sky for a glimpse of a ship or a plane.

Under Alex's instruction, the others had nearly finished constructing A-frame beds, which were raised above the ground to keep them clear of sandflies, centipedes and scorpions. First they had made the head and foot of the beds by driving two pairs of bamboo posts into the sand at an angle and lashing the tops together with split vines. The beds themselves were two long bamboo poles with a mattress of cross-woven vines holding the poles together. Once the beds were finished it was a simple matter to slide the ends of the long poles down the outside of the two A-frames until the vine mattress was pulled taut, leaving the bed suspended well above the ground.

'How are those coconut drinks coming along, Hex?' called Alex, as he and Paulo slotted the last bed into place on its A-frame. 'We're about ready for a break.'

Hex had been using a sharpened bamboo stake to

break open the husks of five coconuts. Then he had wedged each coconut into the sand and hammered a sharp stone into one of the black eyes until it pierced through to the sweet milk inside.

'All done,' said Hex, handing round the coconuts.

They sat down, tipped up the coconuts and let the milk pour into their mouths.

'Good,' said Li, briefly, wiping her mouth with the back of her hand before tipping up the nut again for another swig.

'Take your time,' warned Alex. 'Too much too fast and you might be sick.' He laid his coconut aside and checked the wooden handles on the flexible saw. They were holding up well so he put that back into his belt pouch and took out his knife. It was a good, strong, single-bladed knife with a wooden handle and it had been invaluable throughout the afternoon's work. Alex inspected the blade, then took out his piece of sandstone and began to sharpen the knife.

'Didn't you just do that, like, an hour ago?' asked Amber.

'You have to look after your knife,' said Alex,

calmly, steadily honing the blade. 'It's the most important tool you have in a situation like this.'

Paulo finished his drink, then took one of the bunk blankets, spread it across the vine mattress of his bed and lay down with a satisfied groan.

'Don't get too comfortable,' said Alex, glancing at his watch and the position of the sun. 'There's a lot more to do before sunset.'

They cooled off with a quick dip in the lagoon then went back to work, wearing the sun-hats Amber had made. Before he left the fire, Alex smashed open the coconut shells for Amber and showed her how to heat the chopped meat by laying it on a flat stone next to the fire. He picked up one of the empty coconut half-shells and handed it to Amber.

'Once the oil starts coming out of the coconut meat and running off the edge of the stone here,' explained Alex, 'you collect it in this half-shell.'

'What's the point of that?' asked Amber, suspiciously. 'Are you sure you're not just finding stuff for me to do, to make me feel better?'

'Definitely not,' said Alex. 'We really do need as much oil as you can collect. It has lots of uses. We can smear it on and it'll protect our skin from the sun and keep the mosquitoes away. And if we mix it with wood ash, it turns into soap.'

'Cool,' said Amber, happily settling to her task.

By the end of the afternoon, the camp was finished. They had rigged up five shelters over the beds, each made from a frame of bamboo poles lashed together, with a thatch of banana leaves and palm fronds. There was even a little shelter over the woodpile for the campfire. Next to the fire, there were two simple, bamboo benches, again set under their own, thatched shelters.

They sat on the two benches, looking around the camp in quiet satisfaction. Two more crabs were cooking in the storage tin over the fire and Paulo had packed the top sections of three green bamboo canes with young bamboo shoots and leaned them over the fire. The lower sections were full of seawater, which was just coming to the boil.

'They will cook in the steam,' said Paulo. 'Beautiful. Like asparagus.'

'If Heather could see us now,' giggled Li, gazing around the camp, 'she wouldn't believe it!'

'We're nearly ready for the night,' said Alex. 'Just a couple more things to do.'

Carefully, he filled a coconut half-shell with boiled water and added potassium permanganate from his medical kit until the water turned deep pink. 'Antiseptic,' he explained. 'In the tropics, a wound'll get infected very easily. So, anyone with cuts, grazes, burns or mosquito bites, step forward.'

'Yeah, well that's all of us!' laughed Amber.

'OK, we'll start with you, Amber,' said Alex. 'It's even more important for diabetics to make sure a wound heals properly. And we need to check for chiggers, too, so everybody take your boots off.'

'What the hell are chiggers?' asked Hex.

'They're a type of flea,' explained Alex. 'Chigoes is the proper name for them. They attach themselves to the shafts of hairs on your skin, then they feed off you by injecting saliva under the skin then sucking—'

'OK,' said Amber, hastily, 'I get the idea.'

'If you don't winkle them out, the bite'll become infected.' Alex had removed his boots and socks and was checking his feet and ankles. He pointed to three red dots just above his ankle bone. 'There.

Chiggers. If we had some vaseline, I could smear some on and suffocate them. As it is, I'll have to use a sterilized needle to dig them out.'

'OK. Now I'm really grossed out,' said Amber.

'Is everything on this island out to get us?' groaned Hex.

Alex grinned. 'Just keep your boots on during the day, wash your socks every night, and you should avoid getting too many of them.'

They took it in turn to bathe their scrapes and bites and remove any chiggers while the food cooked. Li gave Alex's raw wrist and head wound extra attention, but both wounds seemed to be healing well.

Next Alex produced a small pack of anti-malaria tablets. 'These are special,' he said. 'They're not like the ones they were doling out every day on the *Phoenix*. You only need to take one and you have protection against malaria for a month. I have just enough for one each.

'And finally,' said Alex, once they had taken the tablets, 'we have the coconut oil.' Carefully, he picked up the two half-shells that Amber had managed to collect and handed one to each bench. 'Smear it on any exposed flesh. The smoke from the fire'll keep some of the mosquitoes away, but this'll deter the rest.'

'Can't we do it after we eat?' asked Paulo, gazing longingly at the steaming bamboo tubes.

'Nope. This is important. It's something we need to do every night. If we don't keep clean in humid heat like this, we've had it.'

The food was wonderful. To drink, they had half coconuts full of fresh boiled water. Alex crumbled a salt tablet into it before he served it out, to make sure everyone replaced the salt they had lost through the hot, sweaty day. They finished off the meal with the pawpaw fruit which Amber and Li had brought back with them that morning. It tasted rather like a melon and the soft flesh was full of juice. Once the pawpaw had all disappeared, they sat back in a tired, companionable silence, staring into the fire as the sun began to set behind the mountain. After a few minutes, Amber got up quietly and headed down to the tide line, where she sat with her back to them.

'Is she all right?' Alex asked, looking at Li.

'I think she's gone to do her injection,' said Li. 'Best leave her to it.'

'Poor kid,' muttered Hex to himself. The others looked at him in surprise. 'What?' he demanded, scowling fiercely.

'How did her parents die?' asked Li, looking at Hex with frank curiosity.

'Plane crash,' he answered. 'Just over a year ago. It was a small, private plane, with just the two of them in it. Her dad was piloting. Amber was due to fly with them, but changed her mind at the last minute and stayed on with friends instead. One of the engines caught fire over the Alps, and the plane crashed into the side of a mountain.'

'Did they find the bodies?' asked Paulo.

'Yeah,' said Hex. 'Apparently, they were badly burned. From what I read, the authorities wouldn't let Amber see them.' He frowned. 'Maybe that's why she's having a hard time moving on. You know that twist of gold she wears around her neck? Shaped like a broken circle?'

'Yes,' said Alex. 'Does it have some special meaning?'

Hex hesitated. 'I think so,' he said. 'That's an Omega sign.'

'Omega?' asked Li.

'It's the last letter in the Greek alphabet. Omega. The End.'

'The end of what?' asked Paulo.

Hex rubbed his nose while he tried to think of the right words to explain. 'Remember, back on the *Phoenix*, she said she didn't want a new beginning? She said her parents were dead. The End. Remember?'

Hex looked around at the others and they all nodded. 'And have you noticed how the gold is all rough and unpolished, as though it was beaten into shape? I think that golden Omega sign was probably made by hammering her parents' wedding rings together. The End. Do you see what I'm getting at? Amber can't move on. She doesn't want to.'

'Ten out of ten, code boy,' said Amber, softly, making Hex jump. 'I forgot, you're pretty good at puzzles, aren't you?' She moved into the circle of firelight and sat down on the bench, giving Hex a cool stare.

'So, I guessed right?' asked Hex.

'Yeah,' said Amber. 'You guessed right, code boy. But there is one thing you're wrong about.'

'What's that?' asked Hex.

'Back on the *Phoenix* you accused me of thinking money fixes everything.' Amber held out the golden Omega sign so that it glittered dully in the firelight. She looked at Hex with eyes full of a deep sadness. 'So, you tell me, Hex. How does money fix this?'

FOURTEEN

Paulo was deeply asleep, lying flat on his back, when his bed started shaking. He tried to ignore it, but the shaking persisted. Then something light and feathery stroked a ticklish path back and forth across his face. He groaned and opened his eyes. Li was bending over him, tickling him under the chin with a handful of her long, black hair.

'C'mon, sleepyhead,' she whispered. 'Time to get up. You're on breakfast duty.'

'Go 'way,' muttered Paulo and closed his eyes again. They had all gone to bed with the sunset, exhausted by the day's activities and subdued by Amber's sad face, but Paulo's sleep had been broken when Alex woke him in the middle of the night to take his turn on watch. Now, all he wanted to do was sleep for another ten hours.

'Wakey wakey,' persisted Li, moving the hank of hair round to Paulo's ear. He did not shift. 'OK,' warned Li, 'I'm going for the belly now, so you'd better move.'

She lifted the hem of Paulo's T-shirt, then froze, eyes wide, staring down at his stomach. 'Paulo,' she said, quietly. 'Don't move.'

'Move, do not move,' grumbled Paulo, starting to turn onto his side. 'Make up your mind—'

'I said, don't move!'

Li's voice was sharp with urgency and suddenly Paulo was fully awake. He could feel something lying heavily on his stomach. Slowly he raised his head to see what was there. Equally slowly, Li eased his T-shirt away from his stomach and folded it back onto his chest.

For two seconds, Paulo stared at the sleeping snake coiled on his belly. He wanted to jump up and knock it away from him, but he forced himself to stay calm while he tried to identify it. The snake was about the same length as his arm. The head was small and the body was ringed with thick, alternating, black and white bands.

Paulo closed his eyes and took a slow breath. He was almost sure the snake was a small krait. The only thing he had going for him was that kraits were rarely aggressive. They had no need to be. Their bite was fatal.

'Krait?' he breathed, looking up at Li.

She nodded, staring at the snake with big eyes. 'What shall I do?'

'Step back,' whispered Paulo. 'Then make some noise.'

Carefully, Li moved backwards, one step at a time. She reached the campfire and picked up the storage tin and a coconut shell.

'Sure?' she whispered, looking uncertainly at Paulo. He gave the faintest of nods and she started bashing the coconut shell against the side of the tin. The snake stirred. It reared its head and turned, focusing its beady, black eyes on Li.

The other three woke up, complaining about the noise as Li continued to bash the tin. Li pointed to Paulo and, one by one, they saw the snake and froze.

The krait uncoiled and darted its head back and forth. It was disturbed by the noise, but reluctant to abandon the warm spot it had found. It moved up onto Paulo's chest and looked down into his face. The forked tongue flickered in and out of its mouth as it tested the air. Paulo held his breath but he could not stop his heart from pounding and his chest jumped under the snake with every beat. Finally, the krait decided it was time to move on. With one fluid motion, it slid down onto the sand and slithered away into the forest.

'So, it's true,' drawled Hex, into the stunned silence. 'Paulo really doesn't care what he sleeps with.'

Ten minutes later, Alex, Li and Hex were threading their way single file along the game trail that led through the forest to the pool. They carried stout sticks and Hex and Alex had a rucksack each, full of empty containers. They were out of water and had no option but to return to the pool to stock up, leaving Amber and Paulo behind on watch and breakfast duty.

Moving quickly and quietly, the three of them checked from left to right as they hurried along the trail, but the early morning forest was quiet and they reached the pool without meeting anything.

Outside the cave, the insect cleaning squads had been at work. Every remaining scrap of the slaughtered deer had gone and the rock was smooth and clean. Warily, the three of them waded into the pool and began to fill up their water containers, scanning the cave mouth and the forest all the while. Nothing stirred and they began to relax.

Alex and Li were washing themselves under the waterfall when a deep growl issued from the cave in the cliff. Their heads came up and they began to back slowly out of the pool. Alex turned, looking for Hex, but Hex had disappeared. He turned back to stare into the cave mouth, feeling his neck prickle with fear. Had something come out of the cave, grabbed Hex and dragged him inside without either of them noticing? If so, they were facing a deadly hunter.

The growl came again, echoing from inside the cave. Alex moved in front of Li, gripping his stick tightly. Then Hex popped his head out of the cave mouth and grinned at them. 'Admit it,' he said. 'I had you going then.'

'Hex! Get out of there!' yelled Alex.

'But there's nothing in here. It only goes back a little way, then it's blocked by a rock fall.' He turned and looked back into the cave. 'Hang on a minute, there's something sticking out of the bottom of the rock fall. I wonder what it is? I'll just go back in and have a look.'

Hex started to head back into the cave but Alex bounded out of the water and shoved him hard in the chest.

'You will not go back in there!'

'What?' said Hex, looking into Alex's furious face with genuine surprise.

'Grow up, Hex! This is real life, not some computer game! You can't just say "game over" and start again if you get eaten by something or buried under a rock fall! You'll just be dead!'

Hex raised his hands, palm up. 'OK,' he said, backing off. 'I'll leave it.'

Alex slammed an empty bottle into Hex's chest. 'Fill that,' he grated. 'And stay where I can see you.'

Alex led the way on the return journey. He was still angry with Hex and stalked on ahead without looking back.

Hex marched along after Alex, the heavy rucksack dragging on his shoulders and the bottles of water bumping against his back. It sucked, being a castaway. The physical work was no problem – his body was toned and fit from regular work-outs at his local gym – but Hex felt completely out of place in this environment. He could surf the wilder regions of the Net with the ease of a total expert but he knew nothing about how to survive in this sort of wilderness. Over the past thirty-six hours, he had spent most of his time blundering about like a complete idiot and having to be told what to do by some Northerner who probably thought a megabyte was someone who could eat three Weetabix in one go. Hex glared at Alex's retreating back and quickened his pace to catch up.

Li brought up the rear, also wrapped in her own thoughts. She was going through a mental list of the larger carnivores to be found in this part of the world, but still she could not put a name to the creatures they had heard in the rainforest. She was thinking so hard that she did not notice that Alex and Hex were leaving her further and further behind. A twig snapped over to her right, bringing her out of her thoughts. Li lifted her head, saw the distance between her and the boys and was about to break into a jog to catch up when she saw a movement out of the corner of her eye.

She came to a halt and stared closely at the large bush to the right of the trail just in front of her. She frowned. She was almost certain she had caught a movement from the far side of the bush, but now everything was still. In fact, everything was very still and absolutely silent. Li felt the hairs stand up on the back of her neck as she realized that there was no bird noise in this part of the forest. Even the crickets had stopped their two-note song.

Li swallowed and took a deep breath. As she did so, she caught a hint of a smell. A bad smell, like rotting meat. She hesitated, then cautiously took one step forward and bent to peer through the leafy branches.

The smell was stronger nearer the bush and Li wrinkled her nose. There was definitely something there, behind the branches, but the rustling leaves were good camouflage and, at first, Li could not make sense of what she was seeing. Then a single, reptilian eye jumped into focus.

It was looking right at her.

FIFTEEN

Li leapt straight into the air from a standing start as a huge, dragon-like creature burst out of the undergrowth. It pounced onto the exact spot on the trail where Li had been standing a split second earlier, but she had already grabbed a tree branch and was swinging her legs up out of harm's way. She nearly didn't make it. The reptile reared up with amazing speed and she heard its razor-sharp claws scrabbling up the tree trunk towards her.

Li screamed as she scrambled to reach the safety of the higher branches. For one awful moment, she thought the creature could climb trees. She looked down, and relief flooded through her as she saw that its hind legs were still on the ground. It was using its tail to balance as it reached up the tree trunk towards her and it stood taller than a man. Suddenly it lashed out with a powerful foreleg and Li screamed again as a three-inch-long, razor-sharp claw hooked through the hem of her shorts.

There was a yell from further up the trail and Li nearly lost her grip on the branch as the creature dropped back to the ground, ripping its claw through her shorts as though the material was tissue paper.

Alex and Hex were running back to Li and, for a second, the huge reptile stood still, looking up at her then back along the trail, as though it was choosing from a dinner menu. Its eyes were sunk into each side of its long, spade-shaped head. Thick, white ropes of saliva dripped from its jaws and a long, pink forked tongue slid in and out of its mouth. It had a mottled, brown scaly hide, which thickened into ridges at its neck and around the tops of its powerfully squat legs.

'Komodo,' breathed Li and the dragon lifted its head to look at her, as though it recognized its own name. It opened its jaws wide, showing jagged teeth with shreds of meat hanging from them, and gave a hissing roar. A foul stench of rotting flesh rose through the humid air.

Then the creature made its decision. It lowered its head and charged towards Alex and Hex, slinging its legs forward with a rolling gait and raking up the earth of the trail as its claws dug in. The boys came to a halt, then turned back, looking behind them as they ran.

'Don't run! Climb!' shrieked Li. She knew that a large komodo dragon could outrun a human over short distances, and this giant was gaining on them fast. 'Climb a tree!' she shrieked again.

Alex and Hex raced along the trail, trying to spot the branch or vine that would save their lives, but the trees and bushes were whizzing past too quickly. By the time their eyes had registered a likely branch, it was already gone. The komodo roared again as it thundered towards them, its powerful tail threshing from side to side.

'That one!' yelled Alex, pointing to an overhanging branch a few metres ahead. Hex nodded. They jumped for the branch together. Hex swung out of the way of the snapping jaws just in time. Alex was a second behind. With one last, desperate lunge, he grabbed the branch and swung himself up as the huge lizard launched itself at him. He thought he was clear. He should have been clear.

But he had forgotten about the rucksack.

Hex reached down and grasped Alex by the wrist as the komodo clamped its jaws around the dangling rucksack. It roared through its teeth and began to pull. Alex dug his nails into the bark of the branch and Hex held onto his wrist until he thought his fingers would break, but it was no use. Slowly but surely, Alex was being ripped away from the branch. He looked up into Hex's face as he began to lose his grip and his eyes were full of a hopeless fear.

Then Li's stick thudded solidly across the back of the komodo. It hissed as it let go of the rucksack and swung round to face her. Alex fell and flattened himself into the ground as the komodo's tail swung across the trail, narrowly missing his head. Hex jumped down, pulled him out of the way and helped him to his feet.

'Come on, then, stinky!' yelled Li, dancing away, then moving into a fighting stance. The giant lizard charged and she watched with narrowed eyes, judging her moment. It was nearly upon her and opening its jaws wide when she drew back the stick and rammed it straight down the beast's throat. The stick was wrenched from her hands so quickly, the friction took the skin from her palms. Quick as lightning, she twisted away into the bushes to avoid the headlong charge, then she was up on her feet again and running towards the boys, her long black hair flying out behind her like a flag.

'Ruuuunnn!' she howled, her eyes wild. They needed no second telling. The three of them turned and ran for their lives without looking back.

Li was still shivering with shock nearly half an hour later, as they sat on the benches around the fire, trying to decide what to do. Her normally rosy cheeks were paper pale and her high cheekbones stood out sharply.

'It tried to ambush me,' she said, with a shudder. 'I've read about that. They lie in wait until a deer comes along, then they smash it to the ground and disembowel it.' She shuddered again. 'I was the deer.'

'Yeah, well that one won't feel like swallowing anything much for a while,' said Hex, attempting to raise a smile from Li.

'Swallowing,' she said, her face pale and serious. 'That's what they do. They don't chew the meat, they just tear off huge chunks and swallow it down. They have moveable joints in their skulls so they can open their jaws wide to stuff more food in.'

'That's interesting,' said Amber, trying to stop the flow of words, but Li kept talking.

'They can eat eighty per cent of their own body weight in one go. My dad once watched a komodo dragon eat a whole wild boar in seventeen minutes flat. And I mean *all* of it. I would've been gone in less than ten minutes.'

Alex remembered that single, dainty hoof outside the cave. He closed his eyes, trying to block out an image of a komodo dragon with a blood-soaked clump of Li's long, black hair trailing from its mouth.

'The funny thing is,' continued Li, 'they're not even supposed to be here! Everyone thinks they only live on Komodo and a couple of other islands. How did they get here?'

'Well they are here,' said Alex firmly, wrapping a blanket around Li's shoulders. 'And we have a problem. That game trail is probably a favourite komodo ambush spot. Every time we walk along it, we're risking our lives. But our only source of fresh water is at the other end. Any ideas?'

There was silence while they all racked their brains, but there seemed to be no solution. Then Paulo ran his hand thoughtfully over the bench he was sitting on. Alex had split the bamboo poles in half lengthways to make the seat. Paulo studied the split poles and his eyes lit up as an idea hit him. 'I have it!' he cried. 'We build an aqueduct!'

Sixteen

'Sunstroke,' said Amber, flatly. 'He has sunstroke.'

'No, no! It will work!' said Paulo, excitedly jumping up from the bench and pushing Amber and Alex off onto the sand. He flipped the bench over and pointed to the underside of the seat. 'See?'

'Sunstroke,' repeated Amber, climbing to her feet.

Paulo tutted with frustration and began loosening the vine lashing which held the seat together.

'Hey!' protested Alex as Paulo pulled one of the split bamboo poles free, but Paulo ignored him.

'See?' he said, turning the hollow split pole over to

show them what he meant. 'It is like guttering. If we cut and split enough of these, we can run them in an unbroken line all the way from the pool to the beach, using the undergrowth beside the trail to support them. The water will run down the guttering—'

'And we'll have water on tap,' finished Hex, looking at Paulo with a new respect.

Paulo beamed. 'Exactly,' he said. 'On tap.'

They worked along the fringe of the rainforest all morning, cutting down stands of bamboo with the flexible saw and splitting the stems vertically. Amber worked as hard as everyone else, insisting that she was completely back to normal and did not need to rest up for another day. Once they had cut enough bamboo, Alex and Paulo constructed four simple ladder-sledges, using springy boughs of wood as the runners and lashing cross-pieces to them. The cross-pieces gradually decreased in size so that the sledges were broad enough at the bottom end to take a good sized load, but the top was narrow enough for the two runners to be lashed together. Finally, they carefully loaded the razor-sharp split bamboo onto the sledges and tied it down with vines.

'Now, all we have to do is go back in there and rig the thing up,' said Hex, staring into the dark forest.

Over a meal of bananas, figs and coconut milk, everyone agreed that it was not fair to expect Li to brave the game trail again. She was left on Watch Duty next to the signal fire. The other four each grabbed the towing handle of a loaded sledge.

'Ready?' asked Paulo.

'Not really,' admitted Hex, staring into the undergrowth.

'Just one more time,' said Paulo. 'Then we shall have our water brought to us.'

'If it works,' said Amber.

'It will work,' said Paulo, calmly.

'OK,' said Alex, taking a deep breath. 'Let's get it over with.'

They started construction at the beach-end of the trail. Paulo set up a system where two people scouted to the front and the rear and the other two worked on a section of aqueduct. Paulo was right; it was easy to find supporting vines or branches for the bamboo gutters in the dense vegetation of the rainforest and they moved quickly along, slotting the split stems into place and tying them with vines where necessary. They worked feverishly and silently, jumping every time a twig snapped. Every few minutes they would stop and listen, but the rainforest engine hummed along quietly.

'It must be too early for them,' whispered Alex. 'Don't lizards need to warm up in the sun before they can—'

'Shhh . . .' hissed Amber. 'It's moving.' She pointed her stick at a bush just ahead and they all froze in place. The bush was quivering. The leaves shook as something moved under the branches.

'Oh no,' breathed Hex, feeling a cold sweat break out on his forehead.

'Back off,' murmured Alex, gripping his stick. 'If it comes for us, get up into a tree.'

Slowly, hardly daring to breathe, they backed away from the bush. Paulo brought his heel down on a dry twig and it broke with a loud crack in the silence. The leaves of the bush began to shake more violently and Alex lost his nerve.

'Climb!' he yelled.

They all jumped for a branch but Amber misjudged. She missed and fell screaming to the ground.

The bush exploded like a firework as a whole flock of parrots flew out and squawked away into the canopy.

'Well, you did say they hid in bushes,' muttered Amber defensively, as the other three dropped back onto the trail. 'And that bush was moving—'

'You were right to warn us,' said Paulo. 'And do not let that stop you from warning us again. Next time it might be a komodo.'

They forced themselves onwards, moving deeper into the shadows of the rainforest. The sledges became progressively easier to pull as the load lightened and, sooner than anyone had dared to hope, they reached the pool.

Paulo knocked a supporting line of cleft sticks into the open ground which rose to the edge of the pool, and they slotted the last two sections of bamboo into place. Paulo adjusted the position of the final piece of guttering so that it was under the lip of the pool where the overspill water ran down into the rainforest. Then he stood back.

For a few seconds, nothing happened, then a tiny stream of crystal clear water diverted from the overspill and trickled along the guttering. Paulo ran along beside the trickle, watching as it picked up speed and volume, flowing down the bamboo guttering all the way into the forest.

'We did it!' he yelled, running back to the other three. 'It is flowing!'

They danced in a clumsy, sweaty, exhausted circle, then stumbled to a halt and stood there, grinning at one another.

'Tell you what,' said Amber, turning her head to sniff at Paulo's armpit. 'You should get in touch with the military. They could use you as a biological weapon.'

'Bathtime!' yelled Paulo, picking Amber up and running into the pool with her. Alex and Hex dived in too and they splashed and swam in the cool water, washing away all the sweat and tension of the morning.

'Time to go,' said Alex, a few minutes later, turning to wade out of the pool. 'We can check the aqueduct as we walk back,' he said, looking back over his shoulder. 'Sort out any breaks or leaks . . .'

Alex came to a halt as he saw the looks of horror

on Amber and Paulo's faces. They were staring past him to the place where the game trail came out of the forest. He turned and felt his mouth go dry with fear. A komodo dragon, even bigger than the first one, was coming out of the forest towards them.

Alex froze in place. He could have kicked himself for making such a basic mistake. It was so stupid, letting down his guard like that, even for a few minutes. He looked for his stick and spotted it lying next to the sledges on the bank. They had no way of defending themselves. He stayed absolutely still as the huge lizard ambled slowly up to the edge of the pool and dipped its scaly head to drink. Alex saw that the beast's belly was so distended it was dragging along the ground. The komodo had eaten recently, and eaten well. Perhaps, if they stayed very still and did not pose any kind of threat, it would leave them alone.

The dragon lifted its head and gazed across the pool to Alex. He felt a terrible urge to run as the flat, reptilian eyes fixed on him, but he forced himself to stay still. The beast lost interest and turned away, lumbering towards the flat rock outside the cave on the other side of the pool. Alex guessed that it was heading for its favourite sunning spot to sleep off the meal. He felt the tension lessen slightly in his shoulders. There was a good chance of simply walking away from this as long as they did nothing to anger the sleepy lizard. Slowly, he turned his head to whisper instructions to the others and his heart clenched in shock.

Amber and Paulo were there, in the pool behind him – but Hex had disappeared.

SEVENTEEN

Hex stood in the cave beside the pool, waiting for his eyes to adjust to the gloom. The object he had seen poking from the bottom of the rock fall earlier that morning was still on his mind. It raised a question. It posed a puzzle. And if there was one thing Hex could not leave alone, it was a puzzle.

He had left the pool quietly, to avoid a confrontation, but now Alex and the others were forgotten as the rock fall came into focus. Hex's eyes were sharp and hungry as he moved forward, preparing to solve the puzzle. The object was still there, poking out of the rubble, and Hex levered it loose. He studied it for a moment, then slipped it into his pocket. Carefully he grasped the rock that had wedged the object and eased it away from the rock fall. A few small pebbles and some sandy earth showered into the gap, but the fall held. Hex swept the pebbles away and nodded with satisfaction at what was revealed. He stood back and examined the rock fall, choosing the best place to start. He picked a spot at shoulder height, on the far right-hand edge of the fall. Slowly, carefully, he began to clear a way through.

Soon there was a hole big enough for him to squeeze through. Hex boosted himself up onto the rock fall, sending stones and pebbles showering down, and eased himself into the gap. His head poked through into the stale, dry air beyond and he hung, suspended in the darkness, trying to see what lay behind the rock fall. It was too dark and Hex swore with frustration, then a slow smile spread across his face as he remembered that Alex always carried his survival tin with him. One match. That was all he needed. Surely Alex would let him have one match? Hex clambered back down the rock fall and hurried out of the cave.

'Hey, Alex!' he called, squinting in the bright sunshine. 'I need a—'

Hex came to a stop as the huge komodo reared up on its hind legs with a hissing roar. For a split second he stood frozen as it towered over him, then he turned and ran back into the cave. The ground shook as the komodo slammed back down onto its forelegs and charged into the cave after Hex.

'Oh my God!' shrieked Amber. 'It'll kill him!'

Alex powered out of the water and grabbed a stick. Paulo was not far behind. Together they raced around the edge of the pool towards the cave. They could hear Hex screaming. It sounded thin and high over the terrible, booming roars of the dragon. Then another sound rumbled out of the cave mouth; the sound of a great weight of rocks and earth shifting and tumbling.

Alex and Paulo stumbled to a halt as a cloud of choking dust blasted from the mouth of the cave. They stood there dripping and panting, their sticks at the ready as the dust gradually cleared. The rumbling died away into silence and the cave mouth remained empty. There was no sign of Hex or the giant lizard. Amber stumbled from the pool to join them. She was sobbing loudly and the tears were streaming down her face.

'Stay here, Amber,' said Alex grimly as he and Paulo moved towards the cave entrance.

'N-no w-way,' stuttered Amber. 'I'm coming with you.'

The first thing they saw was the tail of the komodo dragon, threshing back and forth just inside the cave entrance. Alex closed his eyes, imagining the lizard pulling Hex's body into bloody chunks and gulping them down. Paulo retched beside him, then swallowed hard and edged further into the cave with Amber close on his heels. The komodo's tail was swinging less now and the movements were spasmodic. Alex frowned down at the twitching tail then steeled himself to lift his head and look into the cave. The tail of the komodo was all he could see. The rest of the giant lizard was buried under a pile of rocks.

Amber gave a yelp as the tail twitched again, scraping against her shin. 'Is it alive still?' she quavered.

'I think it's dead,' replied Alex, nudging the

twitching tail with his foot. 'Those are just nerve impulses. They take a while to stop.'

'Where is Hex?' asked Paulo.

Alex said nothing. He stared grimly at the chest-high pile of rocks and wondered where to start digging.

Suddenly there was a scrambling from the other side of the rock pile and Hex poked his head over the top.

'Game over,' he said, smiling at Alex.

'Hex! Are you OK?'

'Never better.'

'But we heard you screaming,' stuttered Paulo.

Hex pulled a comic face. 'Wouldn't you be screaming with one of those things coming after you?'

'How did you get away?' asked Alex.

'It was a bit dodgy for a while,' admitted Hex. 'I was climbing backwards up the rock fall, kicking rocks and stuff down on its head. But it kept climbing up after me. Its jaws were snapping right at my heels. One of its teeth actually took a slice out of my leg – that's how close it was. Then, the rock fall started to move. I fell back into this bit, and the rocks fell the other way, onto him.'

'Wow!' breathed Amber. 'You were so lucky!'

Hex looked at Amber. He spotted the tears streaking her face and his smile broadened. 'Crying for me?' he asked.

'Eat your heart out, code boy,' she snapped back. 'I'm crying for Godzilla here.'

'What on earth were you doing in the cave, Hex?' demanded Alex.

'Solving a puzzle,' said Hex. 'Come and see.'

They clambered over the rock pile into the dimness of the cave beyond.

'It's a dark hole,' said Amber. 'What's to see?'

Hex pointed to the cave floor behind them. Amber turned, then yelped with shock. A human skeleton was sprawled against the cave wall. The skull was thrown back and the jaw hung open. The pelvis was broken into three pieces and one of the legs was buried under the rock pile.

'It's a Japanese soldier,' said Hex. 'He's been trapped in here since World War Two.'

'How do you know?'

Hex reached into his pocket and pulled out a rusted bayonet. 'This is what I saw earlier today. It was poking out of the bottom of the rock fall. There's a rifle under those rocks somewhere.'

Paulo studied the skeleton. A few scraps of what once could have been a uniform clung to the bones. 'OK, so it is a soldier,' he said. 'But how do you know he is Japanese?'

Hex reached into his pocket again and then held his hand out to them. A collection of tarnished metal buttons, a belt buckle and a cap badge nestled in his palm.

'But the best is over here,' he said, letting the buttons drop and pointing to a metal frame which was propped against the wall beside the dead soldier. Inside the frame sat a metal box, the front covered with knobs and dials. There were sheaves of wires, their rubber covering long rotted away, and a metal crank handle protruded from the side.

'A back-pack radio!' Paulo dropped to his knees beside the box, his fingers exploring the dials and wires. 'We have one very like this on the ranch. It is in one of the most remote bunk houses, where we stay when we are checking the boundaries. It is very old but it still works perfectly.'

Hex kneeled beside Paulo. 'What do you think?' he said, his voice full of a controlled excitement.

'The batteries will be long dead, but we do not need batteries to transmit, only the generator. It is hand-cranked, see?' Paulo pointed to the handle on the side. 'If I can get the generator working just long enough to send a message—'

'There's a morse code key,' said Hex. 'I know morse code. I could send an SOS . . .'

They all shared a look of excitement. Then Hex sat back and winced at the pain in his leg. The gash was deep and still bleeding freely.

'Come on, then,' said Alex. 'Let's get you and this radio back to the beach and get you both fixed up.'

They hauled the heavy radio over the rock pile and strapped it to one of the sledges. Then Paulo and Alex went back into the cave and cut the tail from the komodo dragon with the flexible saw.

'Our next meal,' Paulo explained to Hex and Amber as they slammed the bleeding tail down onto a second sledge and tied it on. 'Trust me. It'll be delicious.'

EIGHTEEN

The afternoon was drawing to a close by the time they arrived back at the beach. Hex was limping badly and the skin around the gash in his leg was looking stretched and shiny. Alex filled up the storage tin from their bamboo aqueduct and put it to boil on the fire. Then he added potassium permanganate from his survival kit and took the steaming, red brew over to the bed where Hex lay.

Carefully he began to clean the wound. Hex barely noticed except to wince and glare when Alex pressed too hard. He was propped up on his elbows, working on the radio with Paulo. Alex frowned at the wound in Hex's leg. Something was not right. The leg was becoming more swollen by the minute and pus was already forming in the cut. He laid the back of his hand against the leg. It felt very hot.

'How're you feeling, Hex?' he said, casually.

'Fine,' said Hex, glancing at Alex with a slightly irritated look before returning to the radio. The back was off and Hex was making sure all the wires and switches were still connected up. His cheeks were flushed, but Alex could not tell whether that was from fever or excitement.

Paulo was concentrating on the generator. He had finished cleaning the rust from all the connections and now he was using coconut oil on the stiffened crank handle. His clever fingers worked on the handle until he could turn it easily. His face was intent, with no trace of his usual wide smile, as he checked and re-checked the connections. He was concentrating so hard that, when Amber laid a hand on his shoulder, he jumped.

'Sure you know what you're doing?' asked Amber, leaning over his shoulder to stare at the radio.

'Shut up, Amber,' said Hex, automatically, arming the sweat from his face as he squinted at the dials. For some reason, he was finding it hard to focus and he had a thumping headache.

Paulo grinned up at Amber. 'My father calls me his *hombre de la maquina* – his Machine Man. I can fix most things. If this radio has even a spark of life left in it, I will find it.'

'Make sure it's on channel sixteen,' warned Amber. 'That's the emergency channel.'

Hex checked his dials, then nodded, his fingers hovering above the morse code key. He looked at Paulo. 'Ready?' he asked.

Alex stopped cleaning Hex's wound and Li stepped closer to watch as Paulo began to crank the handle, slowly at first, until he was sure it would keep turning. 'Anything?' he asked.

'Keep going,' said Hex, staring at the dials. 'Step up the speed a bit.'

Paulo cranked until the sweat was dripping from his face. He was about to give up when Amber yelled, 'Something's happening!'

A light began to flicker behind the clouded dial

window. There was a crackle of static. Then the generator handle began to squeal. Paulo gave it an anxious glance. 'Now, Hex!' he called. 'Send the message. Quickly! It will not last much longer.'

Hex tapped out the SOS signal on the morse key.

Dot, dot, dot – dash, dash, dash – dot, dot, dot.

'Again!' yelled Paulo as the squeal of the generator handle turned into a shriek and a thin line of smoke rose from the box.

Dot, dot, dot – dash, dash, dash – dot, dot dot.

Dot, dot, dot – dash, dash—

The crank handle snapped off with a sharp crack and Paulo fell forward onto the sand. Startled, Hex stopped signalling but Paulo frantically waved him on.

'Keep going,' he snapped, spitting sand out of his mouth. 'There may be stored power . . .'

Hex turned back to the morse key and resumed sending the SOS message, but everyone could tell it was hopeless. The radio was completely dead.

'Maybe that was enough,' said Li, into the silence.

'Two and half SOSs? I don't think so,' said Hex, lying back on his bed.

'It might be,' persisted Li.

'Even if it was enough,' sighed Hex, 'I couldn't give them our position.' He laughed without humour. 'How could I? We don't know where we are!' The smile turned into a grimace of pain as he shifted his wounded leg, trying to get comfortable.

'But what if a – a satellite picked up the signal? The satellite could pinpoint our position, couldn't it?' Li sent Alex a pleading look. He smiled, but did not know what to say. Li was clutching at straws and, in reality, she knew it.

Alex stood up and walked over to the fire. Spitted chunks of the komodo's tail were roasting over the flames. Amber followed him reluctantly. She was supposed to be keeping an eye on the meat.

'Oh, that is gross,' she said, softly, peering down at the pieces of tail. 'Paulo! The skin is splitting open!'

Paulo was still tinkering with the radio, but his heart was no longer in it. 'Good,' he called over his shoulder. 'That's exactly why we've been roasting them. You should be able to peel the skin back now. Cut the meat into chunks and put it into the bamboo steamers.'

'Do I have to?' muttered Amber, gazing with barely

disguised disgust at the pink meat bulging from the split tail skin. 'Give me a hand, will you, Li?'

'One minute,' said Li. She was watching Alex. 'We need to talk,' she said, softly. Alex looked up, saw Li's serious expression, and nodded. Li walked a little way away from the campsite and Alex followed.

'How's the leg wound looking?' she asked, glancing back at Hex.

'Not good,' said Alex.

Li sighed. 'Do you have any antibiotics in your survival tin?' she asked.

'Why?'

'Do you?' repeated Li, biting her lip and looking at him hopefully.

'No,' said Alex.

Li groaned and sank down onto the sand. Her eyes were brimming with tears. Alex felt a cold chill run down his back.

'Tell me,' he said, sitting down beside her.

'If a komodo doesn't manage to disembowel its prey right away, it has another, slower way of killing,' said Li. 'All it needs is one bite. It doesn't even need to be a serious bite. They have special grooves in their teeth. Shreds of meat collect in the grooves and rot – it's a bacteria breeding ground. Even their saliva has over fifty different strains of bacteria – and at least seven of those strains are highly septic. Once an animal is bitten, it may run off, but all the komodo has to do is follow along behind.'

Li looked at Alex and saw in his face that he understood exactly what she was saying.

'Septicaemia,' he said, flatly. 'Blood poisoning.'

Li nodded.

'How long has he got?' asked Alex.

'Without antibiotics?' Li looked over at Hex and felt her throat close up. 'Three days at the most. Probably less.'

NINETEEN

Alex rested his head in his hands. Suddenly he felt very tired. He had worked so hard to keep everyone alive and healthy. All the basic survival problems had been solved. They had established a good camp, with a separate latrine. They had food, water and fire. But this? Alex sighed. This problem was beyond him.

'Alex?' whispered Li. 'Maybe our SOS got through. And maybe they have the technology to locate us just from that message. What do you think?'

Alex lifted his head and stared out to sea. His expression was bleak and a muscle jumped in the angle of his jaw. 'We'll know soon enough,' he said. 'If someone pinpointed our position, they'll be here before nightfall.'

'And if they're not?' asked Li.

Alex shrugged and looked down at his hands.

'Don't,' said Li in a quavering voice. 'Please don't.'

Alex turned to look at Li. Her chin was trembling and her eyes were brimming with tears. 'Don't what?' he asked.

'Don't give up,' said Li. She shook her head and the tears spilled over onto her cheeks. Alex put an arm around her shoulders and she turned her face into his shoulder. 'You can't give up, Alex,' she wept. 'Not you. You're the strong one. You keep us all going. If you give up, then we're all going to end up like – like that Japanese soldier in the cave. We'll all be skeletons, picked clean by the insects—'

Li stopped as Alex grabbed her shoulders, turning her to face him. 'What did you say?' he said.

'I – I said, we'll all end up as skeletons, like—'

'– like that Japanese soldier,' finished Alex. He let go of Li's shoulders. 'I wonder . . . ?'

Alex turned to stare up at the mountain, lost in

thought. His back was straight and his eyes were sharp and focused again. Li held her breath and waited. Finally, he gave a decisive nod. 'Right,' he said, turning to face Li once more. 'Here's what we're going to do.'

'The lizard's ready!' called Amber, shaking the white chunks of meat out of the bamboo steamer onto a banana-leaf plate. 'Yum, yum,' she added in an under-tone as she stared down at the steaming mound of komodo flesh.

'We shall mix it with this,' said Paulo, mashing boiled yams with a stone. 'And pretend it is chicken. It will be fine.'

'Yeah, right,' muttered Amber. She put her hands on her hips and turned to glare at Hex. 'I said, come and get it!'

Hex sat up slowly, then sank back onto his bed. 'Not hungry,' he said, turning his face away.

'Well that's just great,' said Amber. 'I slave over a hot fire cooking a lovely meal of giant reptile and you turn your nose up at it.'

Hex did not answer. Amber tutted and looked

across at Alex and Li. They were still huddled further down the beach with their heads close together, deep in conversation. They had been like that for the past twenty minutes. Li had drawn some sort of diagram in the sand and they were both studying it intently. Li was doing most of the talking, pointing to the sand, then pointing up at the mountainside.

'Hey!' yelled Amber. 'I said, come and get it!'

Alex and Li looked at one another and shared one last nod. Then they both clambered to their feet and walked up the beach towards Amber.

While Paulo and Amber finished preparing the food, Alex poured some boiled drinking water into a coconut half-shell and took it over to Hex. 'Don't you fancy any lizard then?' he asked, sitting on the edge of the camp bed.

'It's not that,' said Hex. 'I don't feel too great.'

Alex laid a hand on Hex's forehead. 'Yeah, I know,' he said, casually. 'You have a fever. Sit up and take these. They'll help.'

Hex dragged himself into a sitting position and Alex handed over two of the precious aspirin from his survival tin. He noted the time as Hex swallowed the tablets, working out when he could safely give him the next dose. While Hex drank the rest of the water, Alex bent to examine the leg wound. It did not look good. The komodo's tooth had opened up a gash starting just below the knee and ending at the top of Hex's walking boot. The wound had partly closed but pus was oozing out from under the forming scab and the surrounding skin was red and puffy.

'So, what do you think?'

Alex jumped and looked up. Hex had finished the water and was watching him with sharp eyes. Alex quickly replaced his worried expression with a bland smile. 'You're doing fine,' he said.

Hex regarded him with a keen intelligence. 'That bad?' he drawled.

'OK. There's some infection,' admitted Alex. 'We'll eat first. That'll give the aspirin time to work. Then I'll clean it up for you.'

Hex again refused his portion of the food, so Amber put it on a flat stone by the fire and covered it with another banana leaf. Alex did not feel much like eating either, but Amber, Li and Paulo were all watching him, so he pushed a chunk of lizard meat into his mouth and forced himself to chew. 'Good,' he said. 'A bit like . . .'

'Chicken?' suggested Paulo.

'Chicken,' agreed Alex.

Paulo and Li both took a bite.

Amber watched them, then looked down at her own portion. 'It's chicken,' she said, closing her eyes. 'It's chicken. It is chicken. It. Is. Chicken . . .' She bit into a chunk of lizard meat, chewed, and swallowed. A surprised smile spread across her face and she opened her eyes. 'You know, that's not at all bad,' she said. 'For – um – chicken.'

They finished off with mangoes and as much fresh water as they could drink.

'You know, things could be a lot worse,' said Amber, settling back on the bench. 'And now we have our very own water supply just up the beach there. It's almost like home.'

'Like home,' agreed Paulo, beaming proudly as he watched a steady stream of water pouring from the last section of his bamboo aqueduct onto the beach. 'We will be fine here until we are rescued.'

Alex and Li shared a look, then glanced over at Hex. He had fallen into a restless sleep. His face was flushed and his hair was damp with sweat.

'What?' said Paulo. 'What is going on?'

'Come over here,' whispered Li, leading them out of Hex's hearing. 'We need to talk.'

Five minutes later, a grim-faced Paulo leaned over Hex and inspected the swollen leg.

'What do you think?' asked Alex.

'We need to get as much poison out as we can,' said Paulo, sniffing at the wound. 'Already it is beginning to smell bad. I think I know what to do.'

He hurried to the fire where Li was trying to comfort a softly crying Amber.

'Come on,' he said as he pushed the remaining mashed yams back over the flames to heat up. 'You must stop crying. Hex might wake up and hear you.'

Amber scowled at Paulo but he was concentrating on mixing a solution of antiseptic. Once he had done that, he turned one of his shorts pockets inside out and cut away the inner lining with Alex's knife.

Amber sniffed a few times, then wiped her eyes.

'What's that for?' she asked, watching Paulo dip the pocket lining into the antiseptic solution.

'I am making a poultice,' said Paulo, softly. 'To draw out the poison. I have done this often with horses when they develop the poison in the hoof. I hope it will work here, too.' He laid the pocket lining on a banana leaf and stuffed it with the steaming hot mashed yams. Finally, he turned to Alex.

'I need something from your tin.'

Alex stared at Paulo, then nodded and opened his survival tin. Paulo took out a foil sachet.

'What's that—?' began Li, then stopped as Paulo split open the sachet and removed a surgical scalpel blade. Li's eyes widened and she fell silent.

'Ready?' asked Paulo, handing the coconut bowl of antiseptic to Li.

Li swallowed hard, then nodded and carried the antiseptic over to Hex's bed. She stroked his face until he woke up.

'Hello, nurse,' he said, grinning weakly. 'Time for my bed bath?'

'Those aspirin must be working,' joked Li.

Paulo studied Hex's face. He did look slightly better. His cheeks were not so flushed and he seemed to be in less pain, but Paulo knew that would only last until the aspirin wore off. It was time to get going.

'Listen to me, Hex,' he said firmly. 'I will clean the wound first with antiseptic, OK? Then I will make a quick cut with this scalpel and put this hot poultice over it—'

'Scalpel?' interrupted Hex, his voice loud with shock.

'I cannot let the wound close up,' explained Paulo. 'The pus has to drain.'

'Are you sure you know what you're doing?' demanded Amber.

'The pus has to drain,' repeated Paulo, looking into Hex's eyes. 'I'll be as quick as I can.'

Hex looked back at Paulo for the longest time, searching his face. Paulo kept his gaze steady. Finally, Hex tightened his lips and nodded.

TWENTY

Hex made no sound when the scalpel went in, but his whole body stiffened. Quickly, Paulo drew the blade down through the crusted scab and the pus spurted out. Hex bit his lip and flung his head from side to side. His eyes were glazed with pain and the tendons stood out in his neck.

'Nearly over,' said Paulo, dropping the scalpel blade into the bowl of antiseptic. He picked up the hot poultice and pressed it over the newly opened wound. 'That is it. All done.'

Hex groaned and relaxed into the bed. His forehead was beaded with sweat and he was pale under his tan. 'Remind me to do the same for you some time,' he panted, glaring at Paulo.

'That was so gross,' said Amber faintly.

'But it's over,' said Hex. 'It'll get better now.' He looked up at the others, gathered around his bed. 'Won't it?'

This was the moment they had been dreading. They all looked down at Hex and nobody knew what to say. Finally, Alex spoke. 'Keeping the wound clean will help,' he said, carefully.

'But . . . ?' said Hex, narrowing his eyes. 'I hear a "but".'

'But komodos have a lot of bacteria on their teeth,' said Li softly. 'Some of those bacteria are pretty bad. They can lead to septicaemia.'

'Blood poisoning,' said Hex quietly. He looked straight at Alex. 'Am I going to get better?'

'Not without antibiotics,' said Alex.

'Do you have antibiotics in your kit?' asked Hex.

'No.'

Hex nodded, then closed his eyes and took a deep breath.

'But we're going to get some,' continued Alex,

firmly. 'Tonight we rest up because at dawn tomorrow, we're leaving the camp. We're going to trek across to the other side of the island—'

'To the all-night pharmacy?' interrupted Hex. 'Come on, Alex. I'm too old for bed-time stories. This island is uninhabited.'

'It is now,' agreed Alex. 'But what about in the war? Think about it! We already found one Japanese soldier. I reckon he was up there on look-out duty. He had the radio to keep in touch with the rest of his unit.'

'So there must have been other soldiers on the island,' said Paulo.

'Exactly! I think they might have had a base or a camp of some sort on the other side of the island. There could be another radio. There could be medical supplies. Antibiotics—'

'Did they have antibiotics then?' asked Hex.

'Yeah, sure they did,' said Amber confidently. 'Penicillin, definitely.'

'They'll be a bit past their sell-by date,' said Hex, but there was a flicker of hope in his eyes.

'Li has already worked out the best route,' said Alex. 'Want to talk us through it, Li?'

'OK. We had a good view of the lie of the land when we were up on the headland the other day. Remember, Amber?'

Amber nodded, although it all seemed a long time ago.

'We can't skirt the coast,' continued Li. 'There are mangrove swamps beyond this lagoon, both ways. Besides, it would take too long. I – I mean—' She stumbled to a halt, glancing quickly at Hex, then away again. 'What I mean is, we wouldn't do it in a day that way.'

'So where do we go?' asked Paulo. 'Through the rainforest?'

'Again, that would take more than a day, and it's very easy to get lost when you can't see more than a few metres ahead. We could end up going in circles. No, I think the best way is up. We should get out of the rainforest onto the lower slopes as soon as we can, then work our way round the eastern shoulder of the mountain to the other side. That way we can see where we're going and the distance is much shorter.'

'Any climbing?' asked Paulo.

'It's mostly just hard walking. There is one outcrop curving all the way round the shoulder to the other side, but I think I could free-climb that, then anchor the rope for the rest of you. Remember, Amber? The way we did it?'

'Yeah. That was OK,' said Amber.

'But we can't just abandon the camp and the signal fire,' said Hex.

'We'll leave a marker arrow, pointing the way we go,' said Alex.

'But we could split up,' insisted Hex. 'Amber could stay here with me until the rest of you come back.'

Alex nodded. He had been expecting this question. The truth was that Hex only had enough time left for a one-way trip, but that was not the answer Alex gave.

'It's not safe to split up,' he said, smoothly. 'Not with komodos hunting in this part of the island. Besides, it's going to take four of us to carry the stretcher.'

'Stretcher?' said Hex. 'You think I'll need a stretcher?'

Alex could have kicked himself. They had decided to keep quiet about how quickly the blood poisoning would develop. Now here he was shooting his mouth off about stretchers. He forced himself to grin down at Hex.

'You mean you don't want to be carried in state around the island, watching the rest of us sweat?'

'I'm not that sick,' said Hex, glaring up at them from fever-bright eyes. 'I'll walk. I'm not too sick to walk. Am I?'

'No,' lied Alex, 'but it would be better to rest that leg.' He started getting to his feet but Hex reached out and caught his wrist in a hard grip.

'You haven't said it yet,' said Hex.

'Said what?' asked Alex.

'Come on,' said Hex, still gripping Alex's wrist. 'Say what you always say. Look me in the eye and tell me I'll live.'

Alex looked down at Hex. He was not sure he could make such a promise. He knew how bad the odds were for Hex. This trek across the island was a desperate measure, but anything was better than sitting back in camp and watching him die. The chances of finding another radio or a cache of usable penicillin were remote, but it was Hex's only hope. Alex concentrated on that hope and pushed everything else to the back of his mind.

'You'll live,' he said, looking Hex squarely in the eye.

'And you always keep your word. Right, Alex?'

'Right,' said Alex.

While Paulo nursed Hex, the rest of them spent the hour or so left before nightfall getting ready for the trek. Amber and Li boiled up water and collected fruit. There was no point in keeping the remains of the komodo tail – meat went off too quickly in the tropical heat – so they buried it well away from the camp. Alex cut a couple of strong, fibrous vines and sat by the fire, splitting and plaiting them into one long and four short lengths of rope.

They worked in silence, each wrapped in their own thoughts. Every now and then one of them would stare out to sea or search the sky, but no rescuers appeared and slowly the hope that their SOS signal had been picked up began to fade.

By the time the sun began to sink below the

horizon, the camp was neat and tidy and the two rucksacks were packed, ready for the morning. Everyone had showered under the bamboo aqueduct and their socks were laid out in a row on the bench in front of the fire to dry. Alex looked around and nodded. He only had one more thing to do, but he had to wait until Hex was asleep first.

'How're you doing?' he asked, moving over to Hex's bed.

'I'm still here,' said Hex, struggling up onto his elbows. His face was flushed and his shirt was soaked with sweat. He grimaced with pain as Paulo gently removed the poultice and checked the wound. The swelling was beginning to spread up the leg and the whole area was red and angry-looking. The poultice had absorbed a lot of the poison, but the cut was full of pus and there was a bad smell coming off it. Paulo looked at Alex and shook his head before going off to make a new poultice.

'Time for some more aspirin,' said Alex, reaching for his survival tin.

'How am I doing?' asked Hex, after he had swallowed the tablets.

'Great,' lied Alex. 'Looking good.'

Alex took the first watch. One by one the other three smeared fresh coconut oil over any exposed skin and climbed, yawning into their beds. Alex sat by the fire, piling green branches onto the flames to create a protective haze of smoke against mosquitoes. He was waiting for Hex to fall asleep. The sun had set and the sudden, tropical night had arrived before he was finally sure.

Silently, Alex picked up the four shorter ropes he had made and moved over to Hex's bed. He stood for a moment, listening to Hex's fever-fast breathing, then he crouched down in the glow from the fire and began the job of converting the bed into a stretcher.

TWENTY-ONE

Li stared up at the cliff face. It towered above her: a vertical slab of dark, volcanic rock rising out of the mountainside. It looked smooth and featureless at first glance, but Li had been studying it for a good five minutes as she planned her route to the top and her sharp eyes had picked out hundreds of tiny ledges and crevices.

A little way down the slope behind her, the others were sitting with their backs against a group of rocks. It was only mid-morning but they were glad of the rest. Drenched in sweat, they had been on the move since dawn, struggling through primary rainforest to reach the lower slopes of the mountain. As well as carrying two rucksacks, two coils of rope and the rolled bunk blankets on their backs, they were also hauling Hex along on a makeshift stretcher-bed. Alex and Paulo had taken the heavier, head-end of the stretcher, with Amber and Li bringing up the rear. Alex had secured his vine ropes to each corner of the stretcher, where they served as four shoulder straps and helped to distribute the weight more evenly, but still the constant friction of the bamboo stretcher poles had rubbed blisters into the palms of their hands.

Li glanced over at the rest of the group, then turned back to the cliff. She mapped the route one more time, turning her head from side to side and squinting as she concentrated.

'Easy peasy,' she murmured, stepping back. She backed straight into Paulo, who had left the others and was hovering anxiously behind her.

'Li. You should not climb first,' he said. 'Not without a rope. Let me climb for you. Please.'

Li sighed. 'Listen to me, Paulo. It was funny on the *Phoenix*. Here, it's just a pain.'

'I am sorry?' said Paulo.

'Stop treating me as though I'm made of glass, Paulo!'

'But I am only caring for you.'

'Don't be ridiculous!' snapped Li. 'I could climb that with my eyes shut, so why not let me get on with it?'

Paulo hung his head. 'I could not bear it if you fell.'

He looked so miserable that Li reached up and put her arms around his neck. 'I won't,' she said softly. 'I promise.'

Paulo beamed down at her, then they both went to join the others.

'OK,' said Li, tying one end of the thinner, nylon line around her waist with a bowline. 'Here's the plan. I go first. The rest of you, watch where I put my hands and feet. Once I'm up here, I'll anchor the rope and keep it taut for the next climber.'

'What about Hex?' asked Amber, quietly. They all looked over at the stretcher. Hex was sweating too, but with fever, not exertion. His leg was swollen, despite their attempts to keep the wound as clean as possible, and his face was pale and gaunt.

'That's what this is for,' said Alex, picking up the thicker rope that had originally tied the tender up to the *Phoenix*. 'Once you and Paulo are up there, I'm going to tie one end of this rope to the nylon line and make a sort of a cradle out of the other end for the stretcher to rest in. Then you pull up the thicker rope—'

'And use that to haul him to the top,' finished Paulo, nodding with understanding.

'Good,' said Li. She sat down and began untying her boot laces. 'I'm going barefoot,' she said, hauling off her boots and socks and stuffing them into the top of one of the rucksacks. 'Just to test the footholds for the rest of you. See ya!'

She walked to the base of the cliff and let the coiled nylon rope drop to the ground. Paulo hurried to pick it up and she turned to wink at him then, casually, began to climb. It was like watching a slow dance. Li seemed to flow up the cliff, gripping tiny ledges of rock with her fingers or toes. She moved one hand or foot at a time, then made sure of her holds before moving again. The coil of rope Paulo held grew smaller and smaller as she made her way higher, a tail of rope swinging behind her. In less than five minutes, she was on the mountain slope at the top of the cliff and securing the rope to a large boulder.

The other three shared out the rucksacks and bunk blankets and strapped them on, then Amber climbed next, with Li belaying the rope for her. Paulo followed more slowly. He was not a natural climber, and his arm and leg muscles were shaking with the strain by the time he hauled himself over the higher slopes and collapsed onto the stony ground.

Alex used a bunk blanket and the longer length of vine rope to secure Hex to the stretcher like a baby in a papoose. Hex groaned as the rope tightened over his injured leg.

'Sorry,' muttered Alex.

'You will be,' said Hex faintly.

Alex grinned at Hex, then he tested the knots of the rope cradle one last time before giving the signal to the others to start hauling. He held onto the stretcher until it was above head height, steadying it for as long as he could, then he stepped back and watched as it made its slow, spinning way up the cliff. When the stretcher finally disappeared over the top of the stone outcrop, Alex sucked in a lungful of air and realized he had been holding his breath through the whole procedure.

While he waited for Li to drop the nylon line back down to him, Alex put down another trail-marker. This time he used three small rocks, one resting on top of another and the third placed ahead of the first two to show the direction of travel. He had left direction-markers all the way along the route. Sometimes it was a cleft stick with another stick resting in the cleft, pointing the way ahead. Sometimes it was a clump of tall grasses, tied together in an overhand knot, with the tops of the grasses nodding the way to go.

Alex stared back along their route, visualizing each marker all the way back to their lagoon. There he had used stones to make a large direction arrow in the sand, above the high-tide line. The markers were a way of trying to stop the doubts which were building up in his mind. What if he had made the wrong decision? What if rescuers were, even now, arriving at the lagoon, pulling their boats up onto the empty beach, walking around the deserted camp? Surely they would spot the stone arrow? Surely they would follow his markers across the island? Again, Alex had an image of the rescuers shaking their heads in puzzlement as they left the lagoon behind and headed back out to sea. He groaned quietly. The lagoon was hidden away in a fold of the rainforest, but Alex scanned the sea around it, checking one last time for any sign of boats before they left this side of the island. Then the rope dropped down the cliff again and Alex wiped the sweat from his face and hands before tying the rope around his waist and starting to climb.

Half an hour later, they had made their way around the shoulder of the mountain and were standing on the lower slopes, looking down on the northern side of the island. The south side, with the lagoon and their camp, was now hidden behind the mountain.

'What do you think?' asked Paulo, peering down into the green blanket of rainforest spread out at their feet.

'I think we just wasted our time,' groaned Amber, easing her T-shirt away from her sweaty neck. 'It looks just the same as the other side! And I can't see any camp.'

'What were you expecting?' giggled Li. 'A big sign,

maybe? "Follow the red arrows to secret Japanese wartime camp"?'

Paulo sniggered behind his hand and even Alex could not stop a tired smile spreading across his face. Amber turned her back on them and sat down beside the stretcher to loosen her boots for a moment.

'Li's right,' said Alex, scanning the land below. 'It's not going to be obvious – and it's not going to be out here in the open, either.'

'OK, Mister Clever,' pouted Amber. 'You tell me. Where do we start looking?'

Alex let his gaze travel down to the sea, then he followed the coastline until he came to a V-shaped wedge of blue where the sea showed through the forest. He pulled out his compass and took a reading. The blue wedge was directly north north-west of their position. 'See that?' he said, pointing down to the coast. 'We can't see it from up here, but I think that's a rivermouth. There's probably a cove down there where a large boat could be hidden – and a stretch of beach to build a camp. If I was looking for a good wartime base, that would be it.'

'OK,' said Li. 'I'll buy that. Shall we go?'

'Guys?' said Amber, uncertainly. They turned around and she pointed to the stretcher. Hex was staring sightlessly up at the sky with fever-bright eyes. His skin had taken on a yellow tinge and a red rash had appeared on his chest. Alex hurried over and laid a hand on Hex's forehead. It was burning with a dry heat.

'I'll walk,' said Hex, staring past Alex's shoulder. 'I can walk!'

Hex's eyes fluttered closed again and Amber and Alex shared a look across the stretcher.

'We'd better find this army camp soon,' whispered Amber. 'I don't think we have much time.'

They picked up the stretcher and hurried on down the mountain. Everyone was getting tired now and the stretcher tugged at their arms, threatening to pull them down the slope with it. Soon the muscles down the backs of their legs ached with the effort of holding back but they stumbled on, filled with a new sense of urgency. Gradually the slope grew gentler as they reached the tangled undergrowth of the rainforest fringe. They found a game trail and followed it until they were in the shade of the primary rainforest.

There they stopped and laid the stretcher down while Alex took a reading from his compass. Nobody spoke – they just stood there like exhausted horses, covered in a sheen of sweat and breathing hard. Hex tossed and turned beneath the high, green canopy of leaves. His white face seemed to shine with a pale light in the shadows. Li looked down at him and her lower lip trembled.

'He looks like a ghost already,' she whispered.

'This way,' said Alex grimly, pocketing the compass. He moved off, setting the pace, forcing them on through the forest and stopping only to take compass readings. He had made a promise and he would not give up, even though he could see that Hex was growing steadily worse as the bacteria multiplied in his blood. The doubts were loud in his head, now. If there was a camp, it might take them days to find it. And what were the chances of finding a second radio or some antibiotics? The doubts marched around his head in time with his marching feet until, at last, something interrupted his thoughts. Alex stumbled to a halt and lifted his head.

'Listen,' he said. 'Can you hear – surf?'

At first all they could hear was the harsh breath wheezing in their throats and their own hearts drumming in their ears, but gradually their breathing eased. Amber cocked her head, trying to filter out the rustle of the leaves and the song of the crickets.

'I hear it,' she said.

The canopy grew thinner and sunlight began to filter through as they hurried on. Finally, there was only a thin barrier of undergrowth between them and the sea. Gently, they laid down the stretcher and Alex pushed his way through the bushes, ignoring the thorns. He parted the leaves with his hands and looked out into the bright sunshine. The air hissed through his teeth as he drew in a sharp breath and he became very still.

'What?' said Amber, pushing through behind him, Paulo and Li on her heels. 'What can you see? Is it an army camp?'

'No,' said Alex. 'It's better than that.'

Twenty-two

Alex stood back to let the others see. They stared out through the leaves and their faces slackened with shock. There was the rivermouth, the sandy beach and the sheltered cove, all as Alex had predicted. But there was also something else. Floating in the middle of the cove like a shimmering, white mirage, was a beautiful, sleek, ocean-going motor yacht.

'*Dios Mio*,' said Paulo as he saw the bristling collection of communications masts and aerials rising from the highest deck of the yacht. 'We are saved!'

Alex said nothing. He was too full of emotion to speak. He pushed past the others, knelt by the stretcher and squeezed Hex's hand, trying to let him know that everything was going to be all right.

Li turned her head as she heard shouts coming from further down the beach. Three dark-haired men were standing on the shoreline, waving their arms and arguing fiercely.

'That must be the crew,' said Amber. She cupped her hands around her mouth and took a deep breath, preparing to call out for help. Then her eyes widened as Li clamped a hand over her mouth and nose, stifling the shout in her throat. 'Mmmppllfff!' she protested.

'Shhh,' hissed Li, her mouth next to Amber's ear. 'You must be quiet. Something's not right.'

'You're not right!' whispered Amber furiously, rubbing her crushed nose. 'What on earth—?'

'They're not speaking any of the Indonesian dialects,' said Li. 'They're speaking Chinese.'

'What does it matter where they come from?' asked Paulo.

'Oh, it matters,' said Li grimly, scanning the beach.

Her lips tightened as she spotted what she was looking for. 'Over there. See?'

Alex joined the others as they followed Li's
pointing finger. Right at the top of the beach, on the
fringe of the rainforest, someone had built a large,
bamboo cage. Huddled inside the cage were a man,
a woman, a girl of about eight and a boy who was
barely more than a toddler. The father was slumped
against the bamboo bars at the back of the cage. He
had been badly beaten and his face was bruised and
swollen. The mother – a slim, fair-haired woman –
seemed to be in shock. She was clasping her sleeping
son to her chest and rocking back and forth. The girl
sat at the front of the cage, holding a toy giraffe
made out of brightly coloured plastic tubes. Her
solemn brown eyes were unblinking as she stared at
the three men on the shoreline.

'Who are they?' gasped Amber.

'The owners of the yacht,' said Li flatly. 'And they,'
she added, pointing to the men on the shoreline,
'they are pirates.'

'Pirates?' repeated Amber.

'That's right,' said Li. 'Modern-day pirates. They're

a real problem in these parts, once you move off the main shipping routes. They board stray ships and boats, then steal the cargo or kidnap the owners.'

'Then we are not saved?' asked Paulo.

'No, we are not saved,' said Li. 'They would shoot us on sight.'

At that moment, as though to prove her point, the three men finished their argument. The older two turned away from the younger one and sauntered along to the little motor launch which was drawn up on the shore, and everyone saw the rifles slung across their backs. The younger one appeared to have lost the argument. He walked up the beach towards a pile of firewood, muttering unhappily to himself. Grabbing an armful of sticks, he set about building a cooking fire, sending angry glances back over his shoulder at the other two.

'Let's go,' whispered Alex.

Quietly, they eased out of the bushes, picked up the stretcher and hurried back into the cover of the rainforest. Alex's grey eyes were hard and his face was tight with anger as he stood over the stretcher. Hex lay at his feet, edging slowly towards death while a boat full of communications equipment and medical supplies was floating in the bay.

'Right,' he snapped. 'Li. Paulo. You stay here with Hex. See what you can do for him. Amber, you come with me.'

'Where are we going?'

'We're going to talk to the hostages.'

The two of them hurried silently through the forest until they reached the other end of the beach, then they dropped down onto their bellies and crawled the last few metres through the undergrowth, trying to ignore the thorns digging into their elbows and knees. The cage came into view as they parted the long grasses. It had been set right at the top of the beach, with its back pressing against the undergrowth. The man was still sitting against the bars and Amber winced as she saw that his hands had been lashed to the bamboo poles with twisted wire.

Alex inched to his left so that he was hidden directly behind the man, then he crawled out onto the narrow strip of sand at the back of the cage.

'Don't turn round,' he whispered. 'We're here to help.'

Instantly the woman in the cage jumped to her feet and began screaming out a torrent of French words. The little boy fell from her lap into the sand and began to cry with shock. The two men by the boat looked up.

'Be quiet!' hissed Alex, but the woman dropped to her knees, still shouting hysterically. Alex could only recognize one phrase. '*S'il vous plaît*,' she kept repeating. 'Please, please . . .'

Suddenly, she thrust her arms through the bars and grabbed hold of Alex's hair. One of the pirates threw down his cigarette and started walking up the beach towards the cage.

'Let go!' said Alex, reaching up and trying to prise the woman's hands out of his hair. She would not loosen her grip. Then Amber thudded down onto the sand beside him. She started talking softly to the woman in fluent French. The woman stopped shouting and began to listen.

Alex twisted his head painfully to the side. The pirate was halfway up the beach now. Soon he would be close enough to see them clearly. Alex pulled his head back, tugging hard and, this time, the woman let go. Amber hissed one last, urgent sentence, then she and Alex crawled backwards into the bushes and lay flat and still, peering through the leaves.

In the cage, the woman turned and sat down beside her semi-conscious husband. She was trying to get control of herself but she was still sobbing loudly. The pirate walked right up to the cage and peered in with narrowed eyes. He looked at the sobbing woman, then began to walk round to the back of the cage. Alex tensed as he saw the twin crawl-tracks he and Amber had left behind in the sand. If the pirate saw those, they were in trouble.

Then the little girl stood up and spoke to the pirate. He stopped and looked down at her, trying to understand what she was saying. The little girl pointed to her mother, then acted out a mime. First her arm twisted through the air, imitating the sinuous movement of a snake. Then she became her mother, screaming and jumping about on the sand. Finally she imitated the snake again, moving the other way this time, back into the undergrowth.

The little girl smiled up at the pirate and shrugged

her shoulders. He nodded his understanding, then gave the sobbing woman a disdainful look before turning away and heading back to the boat.

Alex slowly let out his breath.

'The little girl told him it was a snake,' whispered Amber, admiringly.

'Yeah, I gathered that,' said Alex softly. He peered out through the bushes. The pirate was back at the motor launch and lighting up another cigarette. In the cage, the woman had calmed down a lot. The noise had brought her husband round and he was sitting up, listening alertly as the little girl whispered into his ear.

'Ready for a second go?' asked Alex.

Amber nodded. Together, they wormed their way up to the back of the cage again and Amber began to talk.

TWENTY-THREE

'You were right, Li. They're hostages,' announced Amber as Paulo thrust a slice of mango and a coconut shell full of water into her hands. 'They're a French family. Philippe Larousse and his wife, Beatrice. The brave little kid is called Emilie and her baby brother is Robert. Philippe told me the pirates hijacked the yacht in the middle of the night and made the crew bring it here.'

'Where are the crew now?' asked Li. 'Still aboard the yacht?'

'No,' said Amber, reluctantly. 'The pirates tied

them up and threw them into the bay this morning. The sharks got them.'

'But that is dreadful!' gasped Paulo.

'I told you,' said Li. 'There's nothing romantic about modern-day pirates. They're dangerous, greedy men.'

'They're keeping the family alive because they think they're worth a lot of money,' continued Amber. 'They're planning on demanding a huge ransom, but Philippe says the pirates are mistaken. He's a plastic surgeon, not a wealthy tycoon. The boat doesn't even belong to him; he only hired it for two weeks for a family holiday.'

'So what is going to happen to them?' asked Paulo.

'Philippe told me that the rest of the pirates went off in their own boat this morning. They took his passport and his business card with them. He thinks when the pirates find out he isn't a multi-millionaire, they will come back and kill him and his family.'

'Then we must rescue them!' said Paulo.

Alex had said nothing since they had arrived back at the temporary base in the rainforest. He had crouched silently on a fallen tree trunk, staring down at Hex and letting Amber tell the story. Now he spoke for the first time.

'Hex first,' he grated through clenched teeth.

Amber nodded and turned back to the others. 'There's a satellite phone on the yacht. And Philippe told me where his medical bag was.'

'Antibiotics?' said Li, hopefully.

'By the syringe-load,' said Amber.

Paulo grinned, then his grin faded. 'But how do we get out to the boat?'

'The motor launch is out, even if we could get past the guards. Philippe says the pirate leader took the keys with him this morning. There was a big argument about it, apparently. The leader doesn't trust his own men by the sound of it.' Amber shook her head. 'Somebody's going to have to swim out,' she said.

'I'll go,' said Alex, springing to this feet. 'I'll go now.'

'No,' said Amber, quietly. 'I'm going. I'm the best swimmer.'

Alex looked at Amber and nodded reluctantly. He

knew she was right. 'How are you going to do it?' he said. 'There are sharks. And the pirates have rifles. If they spot you—'

In reply, Amber pulled a length of brightly coloured plastic tubing from the pocket of her shorts and held it up. 'It's from Emilie's toy giraffe,' she explained. 'I thought it would make a good snorkel. If I swim under the water with strong, steady strokes, I could probably make it to the boat without the pirates seeing me.'

Li nodded in agreement. 'You might fool the sharks too. It's weak, irregular splashing on the surface which attracts them. If you don't move like an injured fish, they might not be interested in you.'

'That's a comfort,' said Amber, with a wry grin.

'Maybe I should go,' said Alex, uncertainly. 'I made a promise to Hex. I should be doing something.'

'Like I said, I'm the best swimmer,' said Amber, calmly. 'And I know what to bring from the medical bag. And I know how to use a maritime satellite phone. Do you?'

Alex shook his head.

'Anyway, I want to do it,' added Amber softly,

looking down at Hex on the stretcher. 'I know what it's like, needing drugs to keep you alive. Knowing you'll die without that next injection.'

She looked up at Alex and they shared a long look.

'Thank you,' said Alex, finally.

Amber slipped out from behind the cover of the rock and slid into the clear water with hardly a ripple. Immediately, she dived deep and struck out for the yacht with steady strokes. She had stripped down to her bra and pants so there was no waterlogged clothing to hold her back as she arrowed through the water, kicking her bare feet in a steady rhythm. The plastic tube was tied around her neck with one of her boot laces. The other lace held a short but deadly-sharp bamboo spear in place against her outer thigh.

Amber held her breath as long as she could, then she put the plastic tube between her teeth and swam upwards until she was just below the surface with the top of the tube sticking out of the water. Now for the tricky bit. She blew hard to displace the water in the tube, then sucked in a lungful of air and dived again. No bullets snicked into the water above her head. The pirates had not spotted her.

Amber continued towards the yacht, swimming for as long as she could, then rising to the surface for another breath of air. All the while she looked about her under the surface, but she saw nothing except a startled shoal of wrasse and a few curious clownfish. Finally the hull of the yacht came into view. She was nearly there!

One more breath and she dived again, heading for the little boarding platform at the stern of the yacht. She had already spotted that the platform had been left in a lowered position. It would be easy to boost herself onto it then take the ladder up to the main deck of the boat.

In her mind, Amber was already on the yacht and picking up the handset of the satellite phone, so it took a couple of seconds to register the three grey shapes that came swimming out of the depths towards her.

Sharks.

Her heart clenched and she kicked harder in a

desperate attempt to reach the platform. The sharks slowed and circled, watching her. Amber pushed on towards the platform. Ten metres. Nine. Eight. Amber felt as though her lungs were about to explode but, as the platform drew nearer, she began to hope that she would make it. Then the largest shark accelerated smoothly away from the other two and headed straight for her.

Back on shore, Alex, Paulo and Li were crouching in the undergrowth, watching Amber's progress across the cove. Every now and then they would get a glimpse of fluorescent green as the end of the plastic pipe poked above the water for an instant. Then a tiny waterspout would shoot up into the air as Amber displaced the water in the tube before diving below the surface again.

At first they would look nervously across at the pirate guards every time the little green tube appeared, but the pirates noticed nothing and gradually they began to relax.

'She must be nearly at the yacht,' said Alex, squinting as he tried to catch the next glimpse of Amber's makeshift snorkel.

'There she blows!' whispered Li. 'Only a few metres to—' She stopped and her eyes widened with horror as three dorsal fins rose out of the sea beside the yacht. Then one fin broke away from the others and arrowed through the water. The fin sank below the surface. Seconds later the shark began thrashing in the water and a plume of bright red blood rose to the surface. The other two sharks closed in, eager for their share.

On the shoreline, one of the pirates pointed out the commotion and they both laughed as they watched the sharks feed in the reddening water.

Li turned away, burying her face in Paulo's chest. She could not bear to watch any longer. Paulo gazed over her head at Alex and they shared a look of utter desolation. The three of them stood together in shocked silence. There was nothing they could do now. It was over. Amber was dead.

Twenty-four

Amber hauled herself onto the platform at the stern of the yacht and lay there, shaking all over. In the water behind her, the two surviving sharks fought over the body of the third, tearing great chunks of flesh away with their serrated teeth. Amber realized how close she had come to being torn to pieces like that. With a groan, she rolled onto her belly and vomited onto the polished wood of the platform.

She had felt a strange calmness come over her when the shark had moved in for the attack. Freeing the sharpened bamboo spear from the lace on her thigh, she had waited, treading water as the shark approached. She knew she only had one chance.

The shark had homed in on her, then turned sideways, opening its jaws as it prepared to attack. Amber had waited until the last possible second then she had rammed her bamboo spear into the dead, black eye with all her strength. The sharpened point had punctured the eye and kept going into the brain until nearly the whole length of the bamboo spear was buried in the head of the shark.

Blood had plumed out into the water and the shark immediately started thrashing erratically, cockscrewing away from her. Its lashing tail had caught her in the small of the back, knocking her out of the way as the other two sharks closed in to feed upon their former hunting partner. She had surfaced on the far side of the platform, coughing up seawater and not quite believing she was still alive.

Amber waited until she felt strong enough to stand, then climbed shakily to her feet and headed for the ladder. She tried not to think about how she was going to get back to shore. One step at a time, she told herself as she cautiously raised her head above deck level. The yacht was deserted. Amber padded across the deck, being careful to keep out of sight of the shore. She reached the glass doors leading to the main saloon, slid them open and stepped inside.

The skin rose up in goosebumps all over her body as the cool, air-conditioned atmosphere touched her. Thick carpeting deadened her footsteps as she moved further into the room, staring about her in wonder. Watercolours in gold frames hung on the walls of the saloon. Squashy white leather sofas and chairs were arranged around a large, glass coffee table. A huge bowl of fruit stood on the table and Amber felt her stomach growl as she gazed at the clusters of purple grapes and the soft, pink skin of the peaches. Less than a week ago, she would have moved carelessly through this elegant room, hardly noticing the luxury which surrounded her. Now she felt as though she had stepped into a different world.

She shook herself and tore her gaze away from the fruit, scanning the room. There was the satellite phone, on another low table in front of a wall of mirrors, and there was the expensive, leather medical bag, perched on top of the bar in the corner, just where Philippe had said it would be. Amber hesitated briefly, then headed for the medical bag first. She clicked open the locks and lifted the lid, then grabbed a plastic bag full of disposable syringes. Next she selected a box full of antibiotic vials and another box containing ampoules of sterile water and popped them into the plastic bag with the syringes. She knotted the top of the bag, then took the shoelace from her thigh and tied the bag securely around her neck.

Amber snatched a handful of cashew nuts from a bowl on the bar and shoved them into her mouth. Then she padded over to the phone, chewing as she went. She stopped in mid-stride with a look of shock on her face as she saw the tall, black girl reflected in the mirror wall. The girl was wearing nothing but her stained, grubby underwear. She was covered in cuts, grazes, bruises and mosquito bites. Her ribs and hip-bones poked out under her skin and her bedraggled hair dripped water onto her skinny shoulders.

Swallowing the nuts, Amber stared at her reflection in astonishment. How could she have got into such a state so quickly? She bit her lip and tried hard not to cry as, suddenly, the whole dreadful situation nearly overwhelmed her. Turning her eyes away from her reflection, Amber picked up the handset of the satellite phone and stopped again, staring at the illuminated keypad.

Who should she call?

Her mind was a complete blank. Nine One One was no good. That number would connect her to the US emergency services and they might have a bit of trouble getting to Indonesia within their guaranteed call-out time. Amber tried and failed to remember the number of the satellite phone aboard the *Phoenix*. Frantically she scanned the phone base and the table, looking for a list of useful numbers. The local coastguard, maybe, or air-sea rescue? There was nothing. Amber groaned in frustration. This was ridiculous!

She racked her brains and suddenly her uncle's home phone number popped into her head. Amber gasped with relief as she punched the numbers into the keypad with a trembling finger. She pressed the 'send' button and waited, imagining the signal heading up into space, hitting the satellite then bouncing down again to connect with the US public telephone system half a world away.

The phone began to ring in her uncle's house in New York and she hugged herself with excitement. She could not wait to hear his voice. There was a click as the phone was picked up.

'Hello?' she said eagerly. 'Hello?'

It was not her uncle on the other end. Instead she heard the warm, southern accent of his live-in housekeeper. Of course, thought Amber. Her uncle would not be at home. He would have flown out to Indonesia as soon as he heard she was missing.

'Roseanne,' she said, breathlessly. 'It's me, Amber!'

The housekeeper continued to talk. '. . . leave your name and number and we will get back to you.'

It was the answer-machine.

'Roseanne,' tried Amber again. 'Pick up if you're there, will you? It's me. It's Amber.'

There was silence from the other end. Amber stared down at the digital display on the phone base. The time flashed back at her in green numbers. 14:05. Her eyes widened as an awful realization hit her. If it was two in the afternoon here, that meant it was still the middle of the night in New York. Roseanne was not picking up the phone because she was fast asleep in bed.

The answer-machine clicked off. Amber swore and hit the re-dial button. She had to try again. She had to leave a clear message with as much information as she could. Impatiently, she glanced up at the mirror wall as she waited for the satellite to connect her. 'Come on! Come—'

She froze, staring into the mirror. A head with tousled, black hair was slowly rising above the back of the leather sofa in the room behind her. A hand, clutching a half-empty bottle of brandy, flopped into view. Then a second hand appeared, holding a knife with a wickedly curved blade. With horror, Amber realized that the boat was not deserted after all. The pirates had left a guard on board.

Slowly she lowered the handset and placed it gently on the table. Silently she began to edge towards the glass doors that led to the deck. The guard's drunken, flushed face appeared above the back of the sofa, his eyes squeezed shut against the sunlight. He groaned, belched, and was about to sink back down into the cushions, when a tinny but clear ringing tone began to sound from the earpiece of the handset.

The guard's eyes snapped open as Roseanne's southern drawl filled the quiet saloon. 'This is the Middleton Residence. Please leave your name and number . . .'

Amber ran for the glass doors as the pirate launched himself over the back of the sofa at her. The bottle flew from his hand and twisted through the air, spraying brandy everywhere. He thudded to the carpet and grabbed her by the ankle, still clutching the knife in his other hand. Amber stamped on his arm, grinding her heel into the crook of his elbow. The pirate grunted in pain and let go of her ankle, but his knife arm was swinging towards her legs.

Amber jumped high in the air, lifting her heels up behind her, and the knife swished by. She landed, staggered, then righted herself and once again ran for the door. The pirate guard was clambering to his feet behind her as she struggled with the sliding door. She could see him in the glass as he focused on her back and raised his knife above his head.

'Please, please, please . . .' she begged as her sweaty fingers slipped from the door handle yet again. 'Please open.'

The guard charged just as Amber finally got a grip on the handle and pulled. The vacuum seal held for a second longer, then the door slid open and she was out onto the deck. She ran for the ladder but the man was close on her heels. He raised the knife above his head and, instinctively, she ducked down onto the deck.

The man could not stop himself in time. He crashed into Amber, crushing her against the deck rail. His feet flew out from under him and he soared into the air above her crouching back, then carried on over the deck rail and down into the water on the seaward side of the yacht.

It took Amber a while to clamber to her feet and pull some breath into her winded lungs. She looked over the rail as the man surfaced. His face was full of fear as he stared up into her eyes. He looked over his shoulder as a grey dorsal fin rose out of the sea behind him, then he turned back and gazed up into Amber's face, pleading silently for help.

With a sob, Amber grabbed the lifebelt from the deck rail and threw it into the sea. The man reached out and hooked his arm over it just as the great white slammed into his back with its mouth wide open. The jaws closed over his head and chest and bit down. The water turned red as the shark shook back and forth. When it pulled away, the man's head and chest were gone. His arm remained, still hooked over the lifebelt as it bobbed on the surface.

As Amber stood frozen on the deck, the second shark appeared, grabbed the arm and the lifebelt together and swallowed them down. Then both sharks dived, going after the rest of the body. The whole dreadful scene had been acted out in virtual silence.

Amber choked back her sobs as she realized that she had to swim for it – now, while the sharks were still occupied with the remains of the pirate. She shinned down the ladder to the boarding platform and glanced quickly at the beach, half expecting to see two loaded rifles pointing at her. The other pirates were still lounging casually on the side of the motor launch. They had seen and heard nothing.

Silently Amber slid into the water and headed for the shore.

Behind her in the quiet, air-conditioned saloon, the light on the satellite phone blinked as it kept following the redial instruction, connecting again and again to an answer-machine in New York.

TWENTY-FIVE

In the rainforest base, Paulo sat with Li, one arm cupped around her shoulders. Alex knelt beside the stretcher, dipping a corner of the bunk blanket into a water-filled coconut shell and sponging Hex's face and chest with it. Around them, the rainforest engine hummed, but they were silent, apart from Li's soft sobbing and the occasional fever-fuelled murmur from Hex. Nobody looked up to see what rustled in the undergrowth between the forest and the beach. Amber's shirt, shorts and belt pouch had been folded neatly and placed on top of her boots in the middle of the clearing and that sad little pile was taking all their attention.

'Omega,' said Paulo, staring at the little twist of gold lying on top of Amber's shirt. 'The end.'

'Hey,' said a familiar voice behind them. 'What does a girl have to do to get some food around here?'

Three heads jerked up in unison and three faces turned towards Amber, each filled with incredulous joy. A second later, she was squashed in the middle of a three-sided bear hug.

'Whoa! Back off!' she hissed. 'Mind the drugs! Don't squash the drugs!'

'You got them?' said Alex, grabbing her by the shoulders, holding her at arm's-length to look into her eyes.

Amber patted the dripping plastic bag which hung at her neck and Alex took her face between his hands and kissed her full on the mouth.

'Wow!' said Amber. 'I must swim in shark-infested waters more often.'

'We thought you were dead,' said Paulo, grinning hugely. 'We thought the sharks had eaten you.'

'Sheesh,' sneered Amber. 'It'd take more than three

sharks to get rid of me. Now, let me through to Hex. I need to get these antibiotics into him. And I meant what I said earlier. I have to eat. Now.'

Paulo looked more closely at Amber, noting the sweaty face and the greyness around the mouth. 'Me and Li will go and find you something,' he said.

Paulo and Li disappeared into the forest together, grinning back at Amber as they went, still not quite believing she had come back to them. Amber knelt down beside Hex. 'Jeez, he looks nearly as bad as I do,' she murmured, staring down at his pale face.

Alex put a blanket around Amber's shoulders and brought a couple of glucose tablets from her pouch, which she chewed as she prepared the injection. First, she ripped open the wrapping on a disposable syringe. Then she lined up four of the little rubber topped vials which held the antibiotic powder, together with the ampoules of sterile water.

'Is that the right dosage?' asked Alex, watching her work.

'Philippe said to give a double dose to start with. That's four vials,' said Amber. 'Here, break these open for me, one at a time.'

Alex took the four glass ampoules. He snapped the top off the first one and Amber drew the liquid up into the syringe, then injected it through the top of one of the vials. She shook the vial to dissolve the drug into the water, then they did the same for the other three vials. Finally, Amber turned each vial upside down and slowly drew the liquid from each one into the body of the syringe.

'OK,' she said. 'Here we go.' Alex held the syringe while Amber tied the plastic bag around Hex's arm above the elbow to act as a tourniquet. She tapped her fingers against the crook of his elbow until the vein stood out, then she broke open an antiseptic wipe from her own pouch and cleaned the area.

'You sure you can do this?' asked Alex as Amber took the syringe and tapped it to get rid of any air bubbles. Amber gave him her best withering look then bent over Hex's arm. She stretched the skin with her other hand then carefully found a vein with the needle. She pulled back the plunger slightly and gave a satisfied grunt when a swirl of blood clouded the clear liquid.

'Untie the tourniquet,' she instructed. Alex loosened the bag around Hex's arm and, slowly, Amber pressed down the plunger of the syringe. They both watched in silence as the antibiotics flowed into Hex's bloodstream.

'Let's hope that's not too late,' said Amber as she slumped back against the trunk of a tree and pulled the blanket more tightly around her. 'I had a real job picking up the prescription.'

Li reappeared first, carrying a small collection of figs and mangoes which Alex opened up with his knife and fed to Amber. Paulo arrived not long after Li. In one hand he carried a whole branch heavily laden with clusters of yellow, apple-sized fruits. In his other hand, he held a carefully folded leaf.

'I thought these looked good,' he said, dropping the branch at Amber's feet. Hungrily, she reached for a fruit, but Li grabbed her by the wrist.

'Wait a minute,' she said. She snapped one of the fruits from the branch, then picked up a stone and smashed it open. Three large seeds nestled inside. 'Yep. I thought so,' Li continued. 'These are physic nuts. Their seeds are poisonous.'

Amber tutted and pushed the branch to one side with her bare foot. 'What's in the leaf, Paulo?' she asked.

Paulo laid the leaf on the ground and opened it up to reveal nine or ten plump, squirming beetle grubs. 'I found them under the bark of a rotting tree trunk,' he said proudly.

'You don't expect me to eat them, do you?' whispered Amber, staring in horror at the grubs. They were each a good four inches long. Their stubby legs waved in the air as they bent their bodies back and forth. Their white skin gleamed in the dim green light under the trees.

Paulo hurried to explain. 'I ate them on my rainforest trek back home. Our instructor told us they were the best source of fat, carbohydrates and protein in the jungle.'

'And you believed him?' said Amber, swallowing as she watched the squirming grubs.

'But you must eat, Amber,' said Paulo. 'For your diabetes, yes? You wait, once they are roasted—'

'We can't have a fire,' interrupted Alex. 'The pirates might see the smoke.'

'Ah,' said Paulo. 'Well, you can eat them raw—'

'Forget it!' hissed Amber.

Paulo frowned down at the squirming grubs, then his face brightened again as he had an idea. 'Leave it to me,' he said. He emptied the grubs onto a flat stone, then picked up a second stone and pressed it down on top of them. They popped with a loud squishing sound.

'Oh, gross,' said Amber, turning away as Paulo enthusiastically ground the grubs into a thick, white paste. Alex was watching her from his place beside the stretcher.

'What?' said Amber.

Alex hesitated. 'Amber, I need to ask you. Did you manage to get to the satellite phone?'

Amber felt a flush spread across her face. She looked down. Her knees were poking through the blanket and she occupied herself with picking at a scabbed mosquito bite. Alex waited. Finally, she lifted her head again and looked him straight in the eye.

'I goofed,' she said.

Alex, Li and Paulo listened quietly as she explained what had happened.

'Right,' said Alex, briskly, when she had finished. 'Amber, you did brilliantly out there. You've probably saved Hex's life. But, the fact is, nobody knows we're here. We're still on our own. Whatever happens next has to be up to us. So, what are we going to do about Philippe and his family?'

'I have been thinking about that,' said Paulo. 'It would be easy enough to distract the pirates in some way while we let the family out of the cage. But then, where do we go? There's no way we can all get out to the yacht. The water is full of sharks and the pirates have rifles. Even if we managed to escape into the rainforest, we would be moving so slowly that the pirates would track us down in no time.'

'We have to do something,' said Li. 'When the other pirates come back, they're probably going to kill them. Even the children. We can't let that happen.'

'If we could only disable the pirates in some way . . .' muttered Alex, gazing around him. He stopped as he spotted the branch of physic nuts and a thoughtful look came over his face.

Paulo hurried across to Amber, carrying a leaf piled with what looked like balls of pink ice cream.

'What's that?' asked Amber, glaring at him suspiciously.

'This is mashed grubs mixed with mango.'

'No!'

'But it is delicious. Watch!' Paulo picked up one of the pink balls and popped it into his mouth.

'No,' said Amber. 'N – O. No.'

'I think you'd better try,' said Alex, quietly. 'You're going to need the energy.'

'Why?' asked Amber.

'Eat up and I'll tell you.'

Amber sighed loudly, then grabbed the leaf from Paulo. 'Water,' she demanded. Li poured some into the coconut shell and handed it over. Amber took a deep breath, then grabbed a ball, shoved it into her mouth and swallowed it down with a gulp of water. Doggedly she carried on until the leaf was clear, then she flung the leaf away from her and swallowed the rest of the water in big gulps. She wiped her mouth with the back of her hand and glared fiercely at the others.

'Do not ever, *ever*, mention this to me again. Ever!'

'Well done,' said Alex, quietly. 'Now, here's what we're going to do.'

TWENTY–SIX

Alex lay on his belly in the undergrowth. Only a thin screen of high grasses separated him from the beach. Carefully he reached out and parted the grasses with his fingers. Out on the beach, the two older pirates were still down by the boat, playing cards. The younger one was much closer to Alex's hiding-place. He was standing over the campfire he had built, stirring the contents of a large cooking pot. Scattered all around him on the sand were empty, catering-sized cans which the pirates had taken from the yacht.

Alex was close enough to read the labels on the cans. He smiled as he saw what had gone into the cookpot. Beef stew, spicy tomato sauce, anchovies in oil, hot peppers and savoury rice. Good. The hotter the concoction, the better their plan would work. The young pirate scooped out a spoonful of the stew and tasted it. He coughed, then nodded his approval. The meal was nearly ready. It was time for Alex to move.

Directly ahead of him lay the pile of firewood the pirates had collected. Stacked next to it were the wooden crates of supplies they had taken from the yacht. Alex eased out of the sheltering undergrowth on his belly, then, using the crates as cover, he wormed over to the woodpile. For a few seconds, he stayed motionless, his head down, listening. Everything was quiet. He had not been spotted.

Reaching into his pouch, Alex pulled out a handful of tinder-dry kindling and his magnifying glass. He pushed the kindling into the woodpile, then angled the magnifying glass so that a concentrated beam of sunlight arrowed into the centre of the dry kindling like a laser. A thin thread of white smoke began to rise.

The smoke grew thicker, then the kindling burst into flame. Alex blew on the kindling and the flames began to spread to the rest of the woodpile. He watched the fire grow. The flames were almost invisible in the sunshine but the fire had definitely taken hold.

Alex wormed his way back into the undergrowth, then skirted round the edge of the beach to Li's hiding-place further along. As Alex flopped down beside Li, the young pirate spotted the burning woodpile and yelled. The other two pirates dropped their cards and raced up the beach to help him pull the crates of supplies away from the flames.

'Now!' hissed Alex.

Li shot out of the undergrowth and raced for the cookpot at a crouching run. She dived down behind the pot and tried to make herself as small as possible while she fumbled a leaf parcel out of her pocket and opened it.

'Come on, come on,' whispered Alex, from the undergrowth. The pirates were still moving the crates to safety but there were only a few left to go.

Li's hand rose above the top of the cookpot and shook the contents of the leaf into the stew.

'Good,' muttered Alex. 'Now get out of there.'

Incredibly, Li stayed where she was. She picked up the spoon from the flat stone beside the fire, reached up again and began to stir the stew. Alex groaned and glanced over to the pirates. The last crate was being carried to safety. Any second now, they would turn and walk back to the cooking fire.

At last Li put the spoon back on the stone and headed back for the undergrowth, just as the pirates dumped the last crate and turned towards the campfire. Li was still out in the open, in plain view. Alex went into a crouch, ready to fight them if he had to. But the pirates were arguing again and looking back at the blazing woodpile rather than ahead to the campfire. Li somersaulted herself into the undergrowth just as the youngest pirate turned his face back to the campfire and stalked up to the pot.

'Cutting it fine,' whispered Alex.

'I had to stir. He would've noticed it otherwise,' whispered Li.

They crouched together, watching as the pirate picked up the spoon and stirred the pot. Would he notice anything? But the pirate hardly looked into the pot. He was concentrating on sending sullen glares across at the other two pirates who were back at the motor launch. He lifted out another spoonful and tasted, then stopped suddenly and stared into the stew. Alex and Li held their breath. The pirate looked over his shoulder at the other two. They had their heads down, sorting out their cards. The pirate smiled slyly, leaned over the pot and spat into the stew. Then he turned and called the other two to dinner.

Alex and Li grinned at one another, then eased out of the undergrowth. They joined Amber, Paulo and Hex behind the bamboo cage. Amber had already whispered the plan to Philippe while she loosened the twisted wire around his wrists and eased his hands free. Now all they had to do was wait.

'Are you sure those seeds were poisonous?' whispered Paulo an hour later.

'Yes,' snapped Li. 'The oil in them is a powerful purgative.'

'A what?'

'She means it comes out at both ends,' said Amber. 'Am I right?'

Li nodded. 'It's pretty violent.'

Paulo peered out through the bushes at the three pirates. They had finished their meal and were lounging around the fire, smoking cigarettes. 'If it ever gets going,' he muttered. 'Are you sure we used enough of them?'

'Well are you sure you crushed the seeds properly?' flashed Li, glaring at Paulo.

'Yes I did!'

'Calm down,' said Alex, from behind them. 'You should've seen the ingredients in that stew. They must have stomachs of steel. It'll probably take a bit longer than normal.'

The other three lapsed into silence, watching for any sign of the poison seeds taking effect. Alex leaned over Hex where he lay on the stretcher. He had some colour in his cheeks again, his fever was lessening and he was starting to come awake. Alex gripped Hex's shoulder and squeezed. 'You'll live,' he breathed.

'Here we go!' whispered Li excitedly.

Out on the beach, one of the pirates was standing up, clutching his stomach. He leaned forward and vomited onto the sand. The other two pirates staggered to their feet. One clutched the seat of his pants and sprinted for the rainforest. The other one threw up into the cookpot.

'Come on,' said Li. 'They're not going to be noticing anything much for quite a while. It's time to open the cage.'

Alex used his knife to saw through the vine lashings at the back of the cage, then he and Paulo lifted out a whole section of the bars. Paulo and Li dashed in, helped Philippe to his feet, then walked him quickly into the cover of the rainforest. Beatrice followed, carrying Robert. He clung to her neck and his legs were wrapped around her waist. Amber put out her hand to Emilie and smiled down at the little girl. 'Come with me, little one,' she said in French. 'It's time to go.'

They marched as fast as they could. Alex, Paulo, Li and Amber led the way, carrying Hex's stretcher. Beatrice was next, still carrying Robert and muttering '*Merci, merci, merci*' over and over again in a dazed voice. Little Emilie marched along behind her mother and Philippe Larousse took up the rear. He was suffering from the beating he had taken, but the escape had given him new hope and energy and he held his head high as he stumbled along.

It was easy for them to find the way back through the rainforest. Alex's trail-markers dotted the route. The party made steady progress and soon they were struggling up the rising ground which led to the lower slopes of the mountain.

'We'll rest when we get out of the forest,' called Alex and the others nodded behind him, saving their breath for the climb. The leaf canopy became thinner and, gradually, the trees became smaller and more spaced out until finally, they left the dense green forest behind and came out onto the shoulder of the mountain. They found a shade tree and collapsed underneath it.

Paulo pulled three mangoes and the last of the water from the rucksack and shared them out. They chewed the juicy fruit and sipped the water slowly, letting the moisture ease their dry mouths. For a while, nobody spoke. The march through the forest had exhausted them all. They lay flat on their backs, staring up into the leaves of the tree. Robert fell asleep against his mother's side and Emilie came to sit beside Amber, gripping her hand and looking down into her face with solemn, brown eyes. Finally, Philippe sat up with his back against the tree and turned his bruised, swollen face towards them.

'I do not know how to thank you,' he said in accented but perfect English. 'I thought our lives were over. Then you appeared like – like a miracle! I wonder, where did you come from?'

'That's a long story,' began Amber.

'We fell asleep in a ship's tender. It came adrift. We washed up here,' said Alex simply.

'Yeah, OK,' laughed Amber. 'Not such a long story.'

'And what are your names?' asked Philippe.

'Right,' said Amber. 'The guy on the stretcher, that's Hex.'

'Ah, the boy with the blood poisoning. He is recovering now?'

'He's doing fine,' said Alex, looking down at Hex and swatting a fly away from his face.

'That's Alex,' said Amber. 'He's our survival expert. He showed us how to build our camp.' She turned to Emilie, speaking in French. 'Wait till you see our camp, Emilie! We have beds and shelters and even running water!' The little girl nodded seriously.

'OK,' continued Amber. 'That's Li over there. She fought a komodo dragon and won. And that's Paulo. He can build or fix anything. Back at the camp, he built us a bamboo aqueduct.'

Emilie tugged at Amber's fingers. 'He is very handsome,' she whispered in French.

'What did she say?' asked Paulo.

'She said you're ugly and you smell,' said Amber.

'No she didn't,' said Paulo, smugly. He grinned and waggled his eyebrows at Emilie and, for the first time, they saw her smile.

'And I'm Amber. Amber Middleton.'

'Middleton?' Philippe leaned forward, looking more closely at Amber. 'The software Middletons? I thought you looked familiar. I knew your mother and father.'

'You did? How?'

'I spend a month every year as a volunteer, working in refugee camps or in Third-World countries. Plastic surgery is not just about face-lifts, you know. I can help with burns, for instance, or injuries from land mines. A few years ago I was working in Africa. There had been another ethnic "cleansing" and I was working with children who had been scarred by machetes. That is where I met your parents.'

'They were – in Africa?'

'Yes. I admired what they did after they sold the company. They were very brave.'

'Were they?' said Amber.

'Yes. In their fight, they stood up against powerful business cartels and corrupt governments – that was brave.'

'Their fight?' said Amber, struggling to understand.

'They fought for all the little people. Exposing child labour in sweat shops, fighting for human rights. They knew they were putting themselves into danger. I was so sorry to hear of their deaths. Tell me, Amber, have they tracked down the people who did it?'

Amber's eyes grew big and a hand went up to her mouth as she stared at Philippe. 'I don't understand,' she whispered.

'Ah,' he said. 'You did not know. I am sorry.'

A rifle shot broke the silence, sending an explosion of birds winging out of the forest. Alex leapt to his feet as another shot rang out, then a third. He ran out into the open and stared down the side of the mountain towards the cove. He could just see the top of a wooden mast poking above the rainforest fringe. The pirates' ship had sailed into the cove and dropped anchor while they lazed under a tree as though they had all the time in the world.

'They're back!' he yelled, racing to pick up his rucksack. 'And I think they just executed your three guards. Come on! We need to move fast!'

Twenty-seven

They scrambled to their feet and set off round the shoulder of the mountain.

'Hurry,' panted Amber. 'Once we're round the other side, we'll be out of sight. We'll be safe.'

'We should have set a watch,' gasped Paulo.

'I know,' said Alex. He was getting very tired now and making basic mistakes. As he sweated and panted up the steepening slope he felt uneasy. He was sure there was something else he had forgotten – another basic mistake he had made – but his weary brain could not grasp what it was.

He was still trying to figure out what was bothering him when they came out on the southern side of the mountain and stumbled to a halt at the top of the rock outcrop. They dumped the stretcher onto the slope and rubbed their aching shoulders. Hex opened his eyes and looked around him.

'Are we still here?' he said weakly, gazing up at Alex.

Alex grinned down at Hex, forgetting the worrying niggle in the back of his mind. 'You've been further than you think,' he said. 'You've been out of it for a good few hours. We're heading back to the camp now.'

'There and back again,' said Hex, closing his eyes and drifting off to sleep once more.

'Alex, cut this bunk blanket into strips,' instructed Li. 'We're going to be abseiling down and people will need protection against friction burns.'

Alex set to work with his knife, while Li pulled their two ropes from the rucksack. She worked quickly, doubling each rope and then anchoring them to the same boulder she had used earlier in the day. In a very short time, the two abseiling ropes were ready.

'Who's abseiled before?' asked Li. Paulo, Alex, Amber and Philippe all raised their hands.

'Philippe, do you feel strong enough for this?'

Philippe nodded confidently. Li studied him. He was tall with a good physique and stood with a straight back, despite the bruising. 'OK,' she decided. 'You and Paulo are going down first.' Li grabbed the two rucksacks and emptied them. 'You'll be carrying Robert and Emilie in these. Strap them on back to front, so the kids are facing you and there's nothing on your backs for the rope to get tangled in.'

Alex hurried over with the blanket strips and Paulo and Philippe wrapped them around their hands and thighs, to serve as protective padding against the friction of the rope. They strapped on the rucksacks and Emilie and Robert were loaded into them, Robert with Philippe and Emilie with Paulo.

'Look after her,' pleaded Philippe as they each grabbed a doubled rope and stepped backwards over the cliff.

Once Philippe and Paulo were down, Li and Alex rigged up a cradle and lowered Hex down on the stretcher. Amber and Beatrice went next, with Amber encouraging and advising a sobbing Beatrice every step of the way. Finally, only Li and Alex were left at the top.

'You go,' said Li. 'I'm going to untie the ropes afterwards so they can't follow us down.' She nodded over her shoulder in the direction of the cove.

'I shouldn't worry about the pirates too much,' said Alex. 'We're out of sight now. Even if they find our trail, it'll take them hours to follow it.'

'Best to be safe,' insisted Li. 'I can throw the ropes down, then free-climb. Easy-peasy.'

Alex grinned at Li, then grabbed the rope and disappeared over the edge. As soon as he reached the bottom, Li loosened the knots at the top and threw the ropes over, followed by her boots.

Alex and Paulo stuffed the ropes and boots into the rucksacks, then stood back to watch Li's descent. She moved easily, feeling for remembered hand and footholds from her earlier climb, but descending was always a slower process. She was less than a third of the way down when shouts and running footsteps came from the mountain slope above her head.

Li flinched and nearly fell. She gripped the rock with her strong fingers and flattened herself against the cliff. Alex stared up in horror as five men appeared at the top of the outcrop. How had they managed to follow so quickly? With a sickening rush, he suddenly realized what had been bothering him. He should have destroyed each of his trail-markers as he passed them. Instead, he had left every single one intact. The pirates had simply followed the arrows.

One of the men barked an order as Li continued her descent. The men unslung their rifles from their backs.

'Run!' yelled Alex, flattening himself against the base of the cliff. 'Down the slope! Into the forest! Now!'

Beatrice dumped Robert onto the stretcher with Hex, then she and Amber grabbed the head end of the stretcher and Philippe grabbed the back. Together they raced for the cover of the trees, Emilie running along beside them. Alex stayed where he was. He was not going to leave Li now. It was his mistake which had got her into this trouble.

'I told you to run!' he yelled as Paulo slammed into the cliff base beside him.

'I am not leaving her either,' scowled Paulo.

They both covered their heads as a shower of stones rattled down the face of the cliff. Twisting their necks, they looked up. Li was halfway down now, descending with dangerous speed. Above her, the men cocked their rifles and aimed them downwards. The leader shouted again, repeating the same words three times. Li guessed he was ordering her to stop, but she kept going. The leader shouted again and the men fired.

Li brought up a hand to cover her head as bullets ricocheted from the cliff face all around her. She cried out and nearly fell as needle-sharp splinters of rock speared into her cheek.

The leader shouted again and the bullets stopped. Li forced herself away from the protection of the cliff and carried on descending, her face bleeding and her head ringing. She was only a metre or so further down when the shots rang out again. Li flattened herself against the cliff. Again, none of the bullets hit her. The angle of the cliff was too steep for the men to have a good chance of finding their target. But Li was still in great danger. Her head was reeling and she was finding it harder and harder to make her shaking toes and fingers grip the rock.

She started to descend again, then she heard the men reloading above her head. Her courage failed her and she flattened herself against the cliff. Tears flowed down her face and she felt her fingers weakening. Just as she was about to give up, she heard Paulo's voice coming from directly below her.

'Li! Listen to me. Alex and I are right underneath you.'

'I thought you'd all gone!' she cried. 'I thought I was alone!'

'As if we would,' said Paulo, his voice full of affection. Li smiled through her tears.

'We have a blanket ready to catch you,' said Paulo. 'Just let yourself fall backwards. Do you hear me? You are already two-thirds of the way down. It is not far.'

Li hesitated. It was against all her instincts to let herself fall back into space, but the men had finished reloading above her and the leader was barking orders once more.

'Li. Trust us,' called Paulo.

Li closed her eyes, made herself go limp and tumbled away from the cliff, arms outstretched.

TWENTY-EIGHT

She landed squarely in the middle of the blanket. The shouting of the leader became more frantic as Paulo and Alex picked Li up under the arms and ran with her down the mountain slope. Li could only hold her bare feet out of harm's way as they raced towards the shelter of the forest, bullets thudding into the ground and pinging off rocks all around them.

Amber stood just inside the sheltering trees, waving frantically to show them the way to the game trail. They raced towards her and she stepped back as their impetus carried them helter-skelter into the forest.

Alex stumbled in the sudden dimness and the three of them fell full-length into the soft leaves that covered the game trail as the bullets tailed off behind them.

'Here,' gasped Amber, dropping Li's boots at her feet. Li yanked them on and the four of them hurried to join the others further up the trail.

On they went, hiking through the rainforest with dogged determination. No-one knew how long it would take for the pirates to catch up with them. If they were carrying rope, they might be on the trail again very quickly and it would be an easy matter for them to follow this game trail all the way to the beach, even if Alex destroyed all his markers. As he marched, Alex tried to figure out what to do next. He thought about hiding in the forest, but then dismissed that idea. If the pirates found them, they would not be able to run again. He thought of leaving Hex and the children somewhere, but one look at Beatrice's panicked face told him she would not tolerate that. There was a hiding-place behind the rockfall in the cave, but there was only one way in or out. It could equally easily become a trap. He stumbled on, his tired brain going around in circles.

One thought kept coming back to him again and again. If the pirates tracked them all the way to the lagoon, there would be nowhere else to run.

They had passed the waterfall and were on the game trail heading to the beach when the pirates reappeared. Amber heard a shout from behind them and her heart sank. She turned and saw the five men, running towards them along the track in single file.

'They're here!' she cried.

Desperately, the exhausted group tried to pick up their feet and run but all they could manage was a tired shuffle.

'They're gaining on us,' whimpered Amber, glancing behind again. As she did so, her foot caught on a tree root and she fell, dropping her corner of the stretcher. She hit the ground hard and all the wind was knocked out of her. Thrown off-balance, the others dropped the stretcher. One of the poles snapped in two and Hex slid off onto the forest floor, groaning with pain as his injured leg folded beneath him.

Behind them, the leader of the pirates smiled and held up his hand, ordering his men to slow to a walk.

He slipped his rifle from his shoulder and his men followed suit. His smile grew broader as he sauntered towards them.

Alex picked up the broken stretcher and threw it into the undergrowth. He and Paulo each took one of Hex's arms and draped them around their shoulders. Then they pulled him to his feet while Li helped Amber up. They moved on, with Alex, Hex and Paulo at the back, but it was hopeless. The men were gaining with every step.

Alex and Paulo seemed to reach the same decision at the same instant. They shared a look then, gently, started to lower Hex to the ground.

'Don't you dare,' grated Hex, lifting his head to look at Alex. 'I want to be standing.'

Alex nodded and the three of them turned to face their hunters. Silently Li and Amber stopped too and retraced their steps until they were shoulder to shoulder with the boys. Philippe looked back and saw what was happening. Quickly, he ordered Beatrice and the children to carry on, but he turned back and stood at the rear of the group, watching the killers approach with a look of quiet determination on his face. If they were planning to kill his children, they would have to get past him first.

The leader was close enough for Alex to see the gold tooth in the middle of his smile when the undergrowth erupted on each side of the game trail. Two komodo dragons burst from the bushes and slammed three of the pirates to the ground. One of the men managed to roll out of the way, but the dragons pounced on the other two, raking razor-sharp claws across their bellies. It all happened so fast that their leader was still smiling as his men were attacked behind him.

One of the men on the ground gave a high, agonized scream as the komodo dipped its snout into his belly. The other fallen man twitched silently as the second huge lizard tore the flesh from his arm. The pirate leader turned, brought his rifle up to his shoulder, then lowered it again and stepped back, out of the way of the komodos' swinging tails. The two remaining men stared at the carnage for a few, shocked seconds, then ran back the way they had come, ignoring their leader's shouted orders.

Alex was as shocked as anyone by the gruesome sight in front of him, but a cold, determined part of his brain was also looking out for his own survival. That part of him understood that, suddenly, the odds were a lot better. However, the pirate leader still had his rifle and they had nothing but a knife.

'Come on,' hissed Alex, a plan forming in his mind. 'We have to make it to the beach!' They turned and hobbled away from the ambush site. Behind them, the leader of the pirates checked that his rifle was loaded before slowly following.

The sun was low in the sky by the time they stumbled out onto the beach. Alex gazed around him, checking that everything was as he had left it. Quickly, they helped Hex over to one of the camp beds and eased him down, then they picked up the camp bed and carried it behind the shelter of the signal fire.

Alex gathered Beatrice and the children around the camp bed. 'Stay here with Hex,' he ordered, before running out onto the beach again to join the others. They grabbed another camp bed and piled it high with the rocks Alex had used to make the signal arrow. Then Li and Amber carried the rocks behind the signal fire, while Paulo and Hex picked up one of the bamboo benches and a lemonade can filled with coconut oil. Quickly, they hurried to join the others.

When the pirate leader stepped out onto the beach, it was silent and apparently empty. He scanned the stretch of sand, then smiled and headed towards the large signal fire, imagining his victims cowering behind it. These people had been nothing but trouble and he was looking forward to ending their lives.

'He's coming!' hissed Amber.

'OK. Get back under cover,' ordered Alex. He leaned forward and set his flint to the tinder in the base of the fire. It caught with the third spark and slowly the flames began to spread. Alex lined up five spears of split bamboo from the bench, dipped the end of each one into the can of coconut oil, then thrust it into the growing fire. When the end of each spear was well alight, he handed them out to Amber, Paulo, Li and Philippe one by one, keeping the last one for himself.

'Ready?' he asked.

They all picked up a rock from the pile, tightened their grip on their spears and nodded.

'Remember,' said Paulo. 'We must be fast and

loud. Surprise is our best weapon – and he cannot shoot us all at once.'

'Very encouraging, Paulo,' said Li and he grinned at her fondly.

'OK,' said Amber. 'Here we go!'

The pirate leader came to a shocked halt as five screaming people suddenly shot out from behind the signal fire and raced towards him, waving flaming spears. One rock flew past his head, then another clipped his shoulder. He raised his rifle and tried to get one of the people in his sights, but they started to zigzag across the sand as they ran. He took a step back. A third rock caught him full on the elbow and there was a dull crack as the bone split. The leader yelled and his rifle fell to the ground as his arm dropped uselessly to his side.

The pirate turned and ran back up the beach. Suddenly he was not the hunter any more. He was the prey. Behind him, Alex let out a roar and flung his bamboo spear. The leader stumbled as it caught him in the ankle, but he managed to right himself and carry on.

Alex was in the lead and gaining fast when

something whizzed past his head. An instant later he heard the rifle shot. His head jerked up and his heart clenched as he saw the two remaining pirates stepping out onto the beach with their rifles raised. He slowed, and the others slowed behind him. They came to a stop on the darkening beach.

It took the pirate leader a moment to realize that his men had returned. He carried on running for a few more steps before he spotted them. Then he stopped too and turned to face Alex and the others. Alex groaned. This was it. They were out in the open, lit up by a blazing signal fire and there was nowhere else to run. He bowed his head as the three pirates strolled towards him. Suddenly, there was no fight left in him. He could hear his heart beating very loudly as he waited to die. The beating grew louder and louder until it seemed to fill the sky.

The three pirates stopped too, cocking their heads and looking about them. Alex raised his eyes and watched as the sky beyond the headland began to fill with a bright, white light. The beating grew even louder and the trees above the beach began to bend and dance. They were all staring at the dancing trees when three air-sea rescue helicopters cleared the headland and swung in low over the beach. Their powerful searchlights raked the sand and the pirates dropped their weapons and ran for the cover of the forest.

Alex sat down heavily in the sand as the rotors blat-blatted overhead. Amber landed on her backside next to him and threw her arms around his neck. She was laughing and shouting something but he could not hear a word. A few metres away, Li and Paulo were jumping and dancing in the searchlights, waving madly as the helicopters dipped their noses and spread out along the beach, looking for a place to land away from the signal fire.

Alex sat on, gazing at the helicopters as they settled in a neat row, whipping up a storm of sand with their rotor blades. A line of uniformed men jumped from the belly of one as soon as its runners touched down. They ran at a crouch through the sandstorm and disappeared into the jungle after the pirates. There was movement and noise all around him. Amber, Li and Paulo raced to carry Hex out from behind the signal fire. Beatrice, Emilie and Robert ran to join Philippe and the family stood in a tight huddle, hugging one another as though they would never let go.

Alex blinked, then slowly turned his head back to the helicopters as their whirring blades slowed into silence. He watched as the door on the side of the nearest helicopter swung back. A tall black man stepped from the helicopter, followed by a tiny, blonde-haired woman.

'That's my uncle!' yelled Amber and she went running towards the tall black man. Alex let his gaze follow Amber, then he focused on the tiny woman who was hurrying up the beach towards him. His eyes widened as he recognized Heather, their Watch-leader. He struggled to his feet and stood there, swaying slightly as Heather came to a stop.

'Oh, Alex,' whispered Heather as she stared at the pale, exhausted boy in front of her. He was filthy, his clothes were torn and he was absolutely covered in cuts, bruises, blisters, mosquito bites and friction burns. He staggered and she put out an arm to steady him, but Alex drew himself up and stood unaided. A grin spread across his face as he looked into her eyes.

'A-Watch reporting for duty,' he said proudly. 'All present and correct.'

TWENTY-NINE

Twenty-four hours later, Alex, Amber, Li and Paulo walked into Hex's room in one of the most expensive suites of a private hospital in Jakarta. It was the first time they had all been together since the helicopter had set them down on the roof of the hospital the previous night. Hex had been whisked away immediately and the rest of them had spent the night being examined minutely by a whole army of doctors and nurses. They had been hooked up to intravenous drips to replace lost fluids. Blood and urine samples had been taken and tested. Their wounds had been treated and bandaged and they had been injected with a whole list of different drugs against tropical diseases. Finally, they had been allowed to eat a meal and collapse into their beds, where they had all slept for the next fourteen hours.

Now, Amber walked into the middle of the suite and looked around. The place was more like an exclusive hotel than a hospital. The air-conditioning hummed quietly, the floor was thickly carpeted and a scattering of wall lights and table lamps gave off a soft glow.

'Sheesh, Hex!' she said. 'I had to share with Li! How come you get a palace like this all to yourself?'

'He was sicker than you,' replied John Middleton as he emerged from the en-suite bathroom.

'Hello, Uncle.' Amber grinned, lowering herself carefully into the middle of a huge, cream sofa. 'Owww! I have bruises on my bruises.'

Alex moved over to Hex. He was sitting up in a hospital bed with an intravenous drip attached to his arm and a protective wire cage over his injured leg.

'How are you doing?' asked Alex.

'He's a very lucky boy,' said a plump little nurse as she bustled into the room with a tray of glasses and a jug full of iced water. 'We've been pumping fluid and antibiotics into him all night, so he's improved a lot, but it was that first dose which really counted. If you hadn't got those drugs into him back on the island, he wouldn't be here right now.'

The nurse nodded at them all for emphasis, then glanced at her pocket watch and bustled out again.

'I think that means I'll live,' smiled Hex, as the door sighed shut behind the nurse.

'I already told you that,' said Alex.

Li eased down onto the sofa opposite Amber and reached for the water jug. She wasn't really thirsty, but she held the jug between her bandaged hands and filled all five glasses, just to hear the ice cubes clink. 'I can't believe we survived,' she said softly, smiling around the room at the others.

'And if you don't mind,' said John Middleton, sitting down beside Amber, 'I'd like to know how you did it.'

For the next two hours, they talked and John Middleton listened, his face growing more and more incredulous with every passing minute. Hex listened too. There was a lot he had to catch up on.

'You are one incredible bunch of kids,' said Amber's uncle finally when they had reached the end of their story. 'Now, do you have any questions for me?'

'Did anyone hear our SOS?' asked Paulo.

'We did pick up a fragment of an SOS signal,' said Amber's uncle. 'But it was too broken up for us to do anything with it.'

'Still,' said Paulo, settling back with quiet pride and beaming at Hex, 'it worked. Our radio worked.'

'So how did you find us?' asked Alex.

'My housekeeper called me at about four o'clock yesterday afternoon,' replied Amber's uncle. 'Of course, it was early morning in New York. She had been woken by the phone which kept ringing every five minutes. When she listened to the answer-machine, she heard Amber's voice.'

'But I goofed,' said Amber. 'I didn't leave any details.'

'We didn't need them,' said John Middleton. 'We pinpointed the signal coming from the satellite phone aboard the yacht. The Larousse family are fine, by the way. They're in a suite across the corridor there. You can pop in and see them later.'

'So the satellite signal led you to the cove,' said Hex. 'Then what?'

'Of course, when we got there, all we could find were three bodies, lying on the beach. Then we spotted smoke rising from the other side of the island.'

'The signal fire,' said Alex.

'Your signal fire,' agreed Amber's uncle. 'We high-tailed it around the mountain and there you were, attacking armed men with a bunch of bamboo sticks. They caught the pirates, by the way what was left of them.'

John Middleton smiled at Amber, then reached out and stroked her hair. 'Your mom and dad would have been proud of you,' he said softly.

'Would they?' said Amber quietly, clutching the twist of gold at her neck. 'I don't know what would make them proud. I don't feel as though I know them any more.'

'Ah, yes,' said John Middleton. 'Philippe Larousse told me you might be wanting to know a few things.

He told you a bit about the work they were doing, didn't he?'

'Just a bit,' said Amber. 'And now you're going to tell me the rest. Right?'

'That's why they sold the company, Amber. They wanted to start using some of that money to help other people. They wanted to put something back into the world.'

'But aren't there governments to do that? Aren't there charities and human rights organizations?'

'Yes, but sometimes the bigger organizations are helpless. They're all tied down by law and rules and red tape. Your mom and dad, they reckoned they could get past all that.'

'You mean they broke the law?'

'More like slipped past it,' smiled John Middleton. 'As private individuals, they could sneak into places where officials weren't allowed to go. They could take food or medicines in or get video evidence out. You wouldn't believe how much of their covert filming ended up on the international news – and that evidence would force the authorities to take action. Do you see?'

'I guess so,' said Amber.

'I was involved in it too,' said John Middleton. 'But my role was less dangerous. I suppose you could call me their anchor man. Their organizer. I stayed in New York most of the time, but I would arrange visas or money, or make sure they had the equipment they needed.'

'What sort of equipment?' asked Amber.

'All sorts,' said her uncle. 'Covert cameras for undercover work, false identities. Stuff like that.' He sighed. 'I don't do any of that now. They were the heart of it, you see. When they died in that plane crash, that was the end of it for me. It was sabotage, Amber, not an accident like I told you. I'm sorry.'

'Why didn't you tell me the truth?'

'Your mom and dad, they wanted to protect you. That's why they didn't tell you about the work they were doing. It was dangerous work. They didn't want you to be involved in any way.'

'So they let me think they were swanning around the world on a permanent vacation! I wish they'd told me the truth. I could've helped them.'

'Don't be silly, Amber,' said John Middleton. 'What could a fourteen-year-old girl do?'

Amber drew herself up to her full height and glared at her uncle. 'A lot, actually, if you think about it. Nobody pays much attention to kids. I bet I could get into places even Mom and Dad would have had trouble with.'

'Good point,' said John Middleton, looking at Amber. 'But it would be too dangerous, Amber—'

'Hey! I just survived a reef, a komodo dragon, three or four sharks and a whole crew of pirates! What could be more dangerous than that?' Amber sat up straight and gave her uncle a level stare. 'I've decided, Uncle,' she said. 'I want to carry on Mom and Dad's work.'

'What, all on your own?' asked John Middleton. He smiled at Amber indulgently. 'No, you'd be far better off going back to boarding school.'

Amber slumped and her hand crept up to clutch the golden Omega sign around her neck.

'But she wouldn't be on her own,' said Li, stepping up beside Amber. 'I'd work with Amber any day.'

'Me too,' said Paulo, stepping up beside Li.

'I'll go with that,' said Alex, moving to stand on Amber's other side.

'Count me in,' called Hex, from the bed.

Amber beamed at the others as they gathered around her then turned to look at her uncle. 'Well?' she said.

John Middleton gazed at the five of them thoughtfully. 'It's true,' he said. 'I can see situations where a group of kids as brave and resourceful as you could really make a difference—' He stopped abruptly and got to his feet. 'What am I saying?' he protested. 'This is nonsense. Dangerous nonsense. We stop it right here.'

'But, Uncle—'

'I've made your travel arrangements. You'll all be flying home tomorrow to see your families before going back on-board the *Phoenix* if you wish. You'll soon forget all about this and—'

'No we won't,' said Amber and the others nodded.

'We don't want to be split up,' said Li.

'We belong together,' agreed Paulo.

'Uncle, we are going to do this,' said Amber. 'With or without your approval. Think about it! Look at the skills we have between us. Martial arts, computer hacking, survival skills, mechanical expertise, navigation experience . . . So? What do you say? Will you help us out? Be our anchor man? Set up training for us?'

John Middleton hesitated. He looked at Amber's face. It was thin and bruised, but he had not seen it so full of life and energy since before her parents died. 'Well,' he said slowly. 'There'd have to be safeguards. I'd need to give my approval to every mission—'

'Thank you!' yelled Amber. 'You won't regret this, Uncle. You'll see!'

'I'm regretting it already,' muttered John Middleton, slumping down onto the sofa again.

'If we're going to be a team,' said Li, 'we need a name.'

'I have a name for us,' said Hex, quietly.

'Thought you might, code boy,' smiled Amber, coming to stand at the head of his bed.

'Go on then, tell us,' said Li, moving with Paulo to stand at his other side.

'It's not A-Watch, is it?' asked Alex, joining the rest of them.

'No,' said Hex. 'We don't just watch any more. We're a force. A force to be reckoned with. I think we should call ourselves Alpha Force.'

'Alpha?' said Li. 'What's that?'

'Alpha is the first letter of the Greek alphabet,' said Hex. He reached up and gently touched the gold Omega sign at Amber's neck. 'Omega – the end. Alpha – a new beginning.'

Amber nodded, her eyes filling with tears.

'And there's another reason for Alpha,' said Hex. 'It just happens to be made up from the initial letters of our names.'

'Amber, Li, Paulo, Hex and Alex,' said Alex. 'That's amazing, Hex!'

'So,' said Amber. 'Are we agreed? We will be Alpha Force?'

Alex, Li, Paulo and Hex all nodded their agreement.

'Alpha Force,' they said.

CHRIS RYAN'S TOP TEN TIPS FOR SURVIVAL IN TROPICAL CONDITIONS

1. PLANNING AND INFORMATION

If setting out into the tropics, plan ahead as much as possible – we always did so in the SAS – and try to know what you might be faced with. For example, why not try and learn about the types of animals and insects that live there before you go? If you wake up in the morning with a spider walking over your stomach, it would really help to know if it was poisonous or not! I always take a basic survival kit with me if I'm going anywhere my survival might be at risk.

MY BASIC SURVIVAL KIT (stored in a waterproof box or tin)

1. Matches
2. A flint
3. A magnifying glass
4. Needle and thread: several needles, and coarse thread
5. A compass, the luminous button type
6. A beta light: this is a light-emitting crystal the size of a small coin. It's good for map-reading at night and for fishing. Expensive, but everlasting.
7. Beef stock cubes x 2 for drinks
8. Medical kit: aspirin, water-sterilizing tablets, plasters, butterfly sutures (once, I had to stitch up a guy's leg. It had been cut very badly with a machete and we couldn't get medical assistance because the helicopter couldn't come in for two whole days, so I stitched up his leg to stop the bleeding. Eventually, the helicopter arrived and he was taken to hospital where the wound was cleaned and healed); a condom (it makes a good water-bag, holding 1 litre of water), antiseptic cream and cotton-wool
9. A mobile phone, though not in my SAS days as

they weren't available then. Nowadays, though, a mobile can be a life-saver

10. A small pocket-knife

If you make a kit for yourself, let an adult check your kit and that you can handle a pocket-knife.

2. DON'T PANIC

It's easy to panic when things go wrong, but panic wastes energy and helps nobody. Stay calm and assess the situation. Check what materials you have available – wreckage from a boat or clothing, and what is available around you – e.g.: good dry sticks for building a fire etc. Then begin working on the most important things first.

Our basic needs in any survival situation are:

WATER FOOD FIRE SHELTER

3. FIND FRESH DRINKING WATER

Guess how long the average human can go without food? The answer is three weeks. But you can only survive three days without water. (During the Gulf

War, I was in the desert and was starting to deteri-
orate very quickly due to lack of water. Without
water, the body just stops functioning. I started
collapsing and passing out. Finally, after three days,
I managed to find some water to drink in the River
Euphrates, and I started to recover fairly swiftly. As
soon as you give the body water again, you can start
to function as normal fairly fast.) In any survival
situation, finding fresh water is therefore our number
one priority.

TO KEEP FLUID-LOSS DOWN TO A MINIMUM:
1. Find shade. Get out of the sun, and don't lie directly
   on a hot surface; place something between you and
   the surface.
2. Limit your movements (just rest whenever
   possible).
3. Eat as little as possible as food requires water for
   digestion.
4. Keep talking down to a minimum and breathe
   through your nose, not your mouth.
5. Never drink seawater.

Game trails should lead to fresh drinking water as animals also need water to drink. You can spot a game trail by the animal tracks on the ground and the way in which the undergrowth is pushed back by regular passage.

When you find fresh water, do not drink it immediately. There may still be bacteria in the water and you should first boil it to sterilize it, or use water-sterilizing tablets if you have any. A mate of mine once drank unsterilized water and puked non-stop for over forty-eight hours! And if you've got really thirsty, don't guzzle it down, take only small sips or you might just vomit it all up again.

4. FIND FOOD

If you've been used to a couple of good meals a day, a survival situation means you will almost certainly feel hungry pretty quickly. Although you can survive for a long time without food, we do need food in order to maintain energy in the long term and build new tissues within the body.

ON A TROPICAL ISLAND, YOUR MAIN SOURCE OF FOOD SHOULD BE FROM THE SEA.

1. Wait for low tide and then check tidal pools and wet sand. Rocks along beaches often bear clinging shellfish and molluscs. Do not eat shellfish that are not covered by water at high tide, and only eat bi-valved molluscs that have opened their shells when cooked (bi-valved means there are two parts to the shell). And be aware that mussels are poisonous in tropical zones during the summer.

2. Seaweeds can be dried and stored for several months.

3. Coconuts. Watch out for these falling and hitting you on the head! Don't drink milk from very young coconuts (green) or old (dark brown) as these give diarrhoea. And believe me, you do not want diarrhoea when you're a hundred miles from the nearest bit of toilet paper!

Within the rainforest, most fruits will grow up near the canopy.

If you scout around near the base you may find food that animals have dropped such as berries and types of fruits and, in extreme emergencies, you might have to try and climb up to get this. However, if attempting to eat any fruit or berries you find, you need to be very careful not to eat anything poisonous. Better to wait, if possible, for rescue. But if it is a real emergency and you must try eating something, take the time to check out whether or not it is OK to eat. It could save your life! First look at the food and see if it appears slimy or rotten in any way, then smell it (an almond or peachy smell is dodgy), then rub a small piece onto your skin and wait fifteen minutes to see if there is any reaction. If not, rub a piece on your lips, again wait another fifteen minutes and, if no reaction, continue in this way, gradually increasing your exposure. Touch a piece with the tip of your tongue, place a small piece within your mouth but do not swallow. Spit it out after a few minutes, and if there's no reaction, try eating a very small piece, no bigger than your little fingernail. If there is still no reaction, you are probably safe to eat it but, to be extra-sure, wait several hours before trying a larger amount. And remember — only attempt this in a real emergency as it's not foolproof as some people react differently to others. You might know someone who has a nut allergy for instance.

If you have been sweating a lot and begin to feel dizzy, sick and tired, you could be lacking salt. A pinch of salt in a pint of water is enough, but if you haven't got any salt tablets with you, dilute a little seawater in lots of fresh water and drink, or leave some seawater out in the sun so that the water evaporates and you are left with some salt crystals.

5. BUILD A FIRE
A fire can:

– keep you warm and dry
– be used for cooking
– be used to boil water to purify it
– be used as a signal (see Tip 10)

A good point to remember with fire is the fire triangle.

Without one of these elements, your fire will go out.

6. TRY AND PUT UP A SHELTER

A shelter can protect you from the sun, wind, rain and insects. It can make you feel better too and this will help increase your will to survive.

You'll need to pick a site where there's plenty of material to build it with, and remember to make it large enough and level enough for you to lie down comfortably.

Try, too, to camp on the edge of forests so that you can see anything approaching.

Places to avoid building your shelter:

l. Hilltops exposed to the wind

2. Valley bottoms (could be damp)
3. Near tracks that look like ones that animals use
   regularly
4. Always look up into tree canopies for dead wood
   that could come crashing down when it is windy.
   A big branch could kill you!
5. Keep away from solitary trees that may attract
   lightning

One further point: a latrine. Make sure this is some distance away from your camp, downwind. It's not just hygienic; inquisitive wildlife could come and check it out!

7. TREAT WOUNDS AND INJURIES

Even the smallest scratch can cause you problems in tropical conditions. Wash thoroughly in sterilized water, then use antiseptic cream if you have it. And wash your own hands in sterilized water first if you are treating a wound on someone else – it's easy to pass on infection. Don't try and be a martyr; if you have a blister, deal with it before it becomes a problem. In the SAS, we had to cover miles sometimes with heavy bergens (packs) so, believe me, I know all about blisters!

8. WILDLIFE AND INSECTS

Not all tropical islands have komodo dragons on them, but there could be wildlife, and it may not all be friendly. Be aware of noises, be careful when following a game trail, and try not to attract attention to yourself unnecessarily by shouting or moving too rapidly over terrain with which you are unfamiliar. At night, if you are part of a group, set a watch to alert everyone to any possible danger approaching.

In any tropical situation, there will almost certainly be lots of insects. There's not much you can do about it but do try and cover bare skin so that they have less access to your body and – I know it's hard – try not to scratch if you do get bitten, as this will often make a bite itch even more. If sleeping in your shelter, try and organize a way of sleeping off the ground to cut down on the amount of creatures that might treat your body as a stepping-stone. And if you've taken your boots off, shake them out before you put your foot back in there – you could find something like a centipede has decided to make a home for itself in there!

In swampy areas, sucking creatures like leeches could also attach themselves to your skin. They will drink their fill and then drop off. If you try and pull them off as soon as you see them, their heads will become detached from their bodies, remain under your skin and can start up a poisonous reaction.

9. READING SIGNS

Unfortunately, survival situations don't usually come with maps, but there are lots of ways you can find your way about by interpreting the signs on the ground and in the air. And if you explore a tropical island, you can make your own map as you go, marking anything you might want to find again, like a river or a good place for fuel for your fire.

As a general rule, the sun rises in the east and sets in the west. Even if you don't know the exact positions, just this fact alone could help you decide how to position your shelter. And if you know anything about the stars, you can use these to help navigate too.

Look up to the sky, too, and watch how the clouds change as these can give you a very good idea of what kind of weather is approaching. Tropical zones have lots of sudden storms and it can help you to survive if you can predict when bad weather could be coming. A storm is not the ideal time to be climbing trees, for instance!

10. SIGNALLING
To maximize your chances of rescue, build a signal-fire so that, at the first sign of any rescuers, you can draw attention to your position.

Keep green and damp wood/fuel for daytime-signalling as it produces a lot of smoke. Keep dry fuel separately for the night-time as this produces light.

If you can't light a fire for any reason, why not try arranging pieces of seaweed on the beach into a message that can be read from the sky. Or polish any piece of metal with sand so that you can flash light into the sky to attract attention. And morse code is known all over the world.

Dot, dot, dot   dash, dash, dash   dot, dot, dot

● ● ●   ▬ ▬ ▬   ● ● ●

= S.O.S.

BE SAFE!

Chris Ryan

Random House Children's Books and Chris Ryan would like to make it clear that these tips are for use in a serious situation only, where your life may be at risk. We cannot accept any liability for inappropriate usage in normal conditions.

About the Author

Chris Ryan joined the SAS in 1984 and has been involved in numerous operations with the regiment. During the Gulf War, he was the only member of an eight-man team to escape from Iraq, three colleagues being killed and four captured. It was the longest escape and evasion in the history of the SAS. For this he was awarded the Military Medal. He wrote about his remarkable escape in the adult bestseller *The One That Got Away* (1995), which was also adapted for screen.

He left the SAS in 1994 and is now the author of a number of bestselling thrillers for adults. His work in security takes him around the world and he has also appeared in a number of television series, most recently *Hunting Chris Ryan*, in which his escape and evasion skills were demonstrated to the max. The *Alpha Force* titles are his first books for young readers.